THE STORY OF A SUN VILLAGE

I0624920

ÇETİN GÖKSU

Translated and edited by JANE AKATAY

Publisher

Cosmo Publishing

ISBN 978-1-949872-19-4

CONTENTS

A brief synopsis of The Mysterious Garden of the Sun

Explanations and glossary

Chapter 1: Back to the village

Chapter 2: The Sun Declaration

Chapter 3: A Quest

Chapter 4: The Sun Culture

Chapter 5: Tiny Suns

Chapter 6: The Culture House

Chapter 7: Eco-tourism

Chapter 8: A Sun Revolution

The Mysterious Garden of the Sun

Güneş, Gök, Doğa, Su and Ay, a group of five young graduates fresh out of university, who have reunited in their out-of-the-way Anatolian village high in the Caucuses, set out on an adventure that will change not only their lives but that of their rural community, for ever.

On a journey that takes them into the remote forests and mountains above their quiet Anatolian home, they confront many challenges and quite a few scary moments before finally arriving at the Mysterious Garden of the Sun.

While there, they meet some extraordinary characters who teach them about all about a lost civilisation that enables people to live in harmony with nature and the ancient Anatolian philosophy of the sun... a way of life that their country has virtually forgotten...

Armed with this amazing understanding of how life could be, they realise that the time has come for them to share this knowledge with their fellow villagers... and come up with a way of reintroducing this lifestyle to their homeland.

But in a modern world that focuses more on self-seeking energy monopolies promoting oil, nuclear energy and fossil fuels and a love of concrete and consumerism, rather than nature, self-sufficiency, sustainability and traditions that have stood the test of time, their once beautiful village is gradually dying.

How can they possibly manage to achieve such a radical project and bring their village back to life?

Explanations and glossary

The heroes of this story have names that are somewhat unusual but not totally unheard of in Turkey.

Güneş: *"Sun," Göksu is fascinated by the similarity of the words Sun and Son in English and their association with light, a link that he uses to great effect throughout the narrative.*

Gök: *Sky*

Doğa: *Nature*

Su: *Water*

Ay: *Moon*

All these names have great significance, for reasons you will understand when you read the story.

The village in the book is actually *Meşe Köyü / Vartgel* – in the Kaçkar Mountains in the Black Sea province of *Artvin*, close to Turkey's border with Georgia. The author's family originates from this village.

Turkish letters

Although Turkish letters are phonetic, there are several specific to the Turkish alphabet which may present difficulties for the non-Turkish reader.

These are:

C – as in "cep" (pocket) is pronounced like the English 'j' as in 'jump'

Ç – as in "çay" (tea) is pronounced like the English 'ch' as in 'chat' or 'chop'

Ğ – is a sound unique to Turkish. If the vowel before it is one of a, ı, o, u then "yumuşak ge" will lengthen the sound of that vowel, eg. yağmur, ağaç. If the vowel is one of e, i, ö, ü then "yumuşak ge" will be pronounced as "y", eg. eğitim, iğne. Since "yumuşak ge" is always preceded by a vowel there are no words in Turkish that start with it.

I – as in ıspanak (spinach) is pronounced like the English 'i' in 'cousin'

İ – as in İngilizce (English) is pronounced like the English 'i' in internet

Ö – as in ördek (duck) is pronounced like the English 'ur', as in 'fur'

Ş – as in şeker (sugar) pronounced like the English 'sh', as in 'sheep'

Ü – as in ülke (country) is pronounced like the English u, as in 'cute'

Many thanks to the *Turkishbasics* website for this information. To learn more about the Turkish alphabet and Turkish pronunciation visit: http://turkishbasics.com/grammar/alphabet.php

4

Idiomatic Turkish words and phrases:

As in all languages, there are some words and phrases that are untranslatable using a single word.

Here is a list of those that are used in the book – in order of use - with a simple interpretation:

Saz: a traditional stringed instrument rather like a lute, mandolin or balalaika.

Davul: a kind of drum.

Muhtar: the elected leader of a village community.

Çardak: a kind of sheltered balcony, often covered with vines.

Sofra: can either be a low table, often circular, which diners sit around cross-legged on the floor, or an assortment of dishes that comprise a meal.

Usta: a master-craftsman (or woman)

Yayla: The traditional name given to Anatolia's highland pastures, where for millennia Yörük tribes decamped for the summer months, to escape from the sweltering Aegean and Mediterranean coastline with their families and livestock.

Yörük: the generic name given to the traditional Anatolian semi-nomadic, transhumance tribes, social groups from which much of the Turkish population that used to predominate throughout Anatolia but are now few and far between due to government legislation geared at ensuring families became settled and became part of the system.

Hayırlı olsun!: Here's wishing for the best

İmce: a communal form of traditional solidarity

Hoca: Traditional Turkish word for teacher.

Bey: respectful Turkish word for Mr.

Hanım: respectful Turkish word for Miss/Mrs/Ms

Teyze: Auntie (sister of the mother), while **Hala** is the sister of the father

Şimdiden başarılar: It'll be a success

Türkü: Traditional Anatolian folk music

Mani: a recital of poetry or stories

Şenlik: a traditional celebration

Su gibi aziz ol: "Su gibi aziz ol" is an idiosyncratic Turkish expression which is used to thank someone when they give you a glass of water.

Caravanserai: an overnight inn providing simple secure accommodation for travelers, merchants, and their animals.

Hamam:a Turkish bath

Kermes: borrowed from French 'kermesse' which means charity sale of handicrafts.

Aşevi: a traditional eating house where soup and food are served.

Sağolun, var olun: thank you and may you live long

Lokman Hekim: Lokman remedies are folk or alternative medicines named after Lokman (a pre-Islamic sage) and in Turkey considered to be a famous physician. For more information see Luqman:

https://en.wikipedia.org/wiki/Luqman

Tarhana soup: This traditional soup, made every summer all over Anatolia, has a long history and as many 300 variations, according to the region. Ingredients include cracked wheat, chickpeas, flour, yogurt, vegetables, spices and herbs, and the resulting dough is fermented and dried. In some areas, the dough is powdered, while in others it is formed into flat palm-sized lumps. The mixture can be stored for months.

Tarhana soup is made by rehydrating some of the dough with water or stock, to which butter is added, resulting in a tasty and highly nutritious soup.

Boğa güreşi: Bull wrestling. In Turkey, unlike European bullfighting, this is bull against the bull and is performed every June on the Kafkasör yayla (highland plateaux) of the Caucasian region. In this sport, the bulls lock horns according to prescribed rules.

Yağli güreşi: Oil wrestling. This is a traditional sport and an important part of Yörük culture. Men cover themselves in olive oil. Wearing specially made leather trousers, called kisbet, the pehlivan (name given to the wrestlers, which translates as champion or hero) attempts to control his opponent by putting his arm through the latter's kisbet. Oil wrestling can be traced back to the ancient Sumer and Babylon. Oil wrestling is also evident in Greco-Roman cultures.

Konukluk: An important part of Anatolian hospitality where guests are respectfully welcomed into the home.

A brief biography of the author

Çetin Göksu was born in Antakya in 1943. He graduated from Çoruh Primary School and Artvin High School in Artvin, studied at Yıldız Technical University where he received a diploma in architecture, a PhD Diploma in urbanism from the Paris Sorbonne University. Göksu is one of the founders of Karadeniz Technical University Department of Architecture and since 1980 has been a METU Faculty Member. Göksu has published a large number of scientific articles, essays, and academic works on subjects including the sun, culture, and ecological planning.

Chapter 1

Back to the village

A dome of light

The young companions, Güneş, Ay, Su, Gök and Doğa, had lived through some extraordinary adventures. But now they were running down the mountain, singing a Turkish folk song about the sun at the top of their voices. They only stopped when they could see their village in the distance. Taking great gulps of the mountain air deep into their lungs, they gazed at the scene below with longing. It was the same place they had left just a few days before. The same village in which they had spent nearly all their short lives. The place they were looking at was their home and where their beloved families and friends lived.

But, in another way, it was as if they were seeing their village for the first time, or at least through different eyes. The bleakness they had known was gone and a new radiance had taken its place. The village they were gazing at from the mountainside was somehow altered; shining, shimmering. If truth be told, the village had not changed. Of course, it hadn't. Only ten days had passed since they'd left, and the village was the same. So, what if the change was not in the village at all? What if it was simply that, for the first time in their lives, they were beginning to realise how brightly the sun shone on their home?

Güneş was the first to speak: "Look how beautifully the sun's illuminating our village!" he exclaimed. "The sun...It isn't only shining on every tree and every building, and every nook and cranny, it's as if its rays are infusing everything with energy. Why haven't we ever noticed this before...?"

Pointing excitedly, Gök interrupted Güneş: "Look! Look! The village is flooded with light and there's a kind of dome of light over it too. I've never seen anything like it. Could it be a mirage do you think, or is it a miracle?" Turning to his friends, he asked them, "Can't you see it?" They all looked more carefully at the area to which Gök was pointing and indeed, they could now see that there was, most definitely, a brilliant dome of light shining over their village. "Yes!" they exclaimed, "Somehow the sun's shining in a different way over our village. It's got to be some kind of miracle."

"And it's not only there!" Güneş exclaimed. "Look... There are domes of light over other places too: every town and village. The Sun doesn't deprive anyone of its light   unless it wants to. It shines everywhere: sharing out its light and energy over the entire world. But, as you know, there's a special reason why it focuses on towns and villages. Buildings absorb some of the sun's rays and reflect others. This reflected energy, combined with other rays, is especially concentrated on built-up areas, creating these domes of light. But, as we're all too aware, nobody's using this energy."

Thrilled by what she was seeing, Doğa joined in the conversation: "Although I don't really understand it, looking at all the animals and plants, isn't it obvious how they all make the most of the sun? For example, virtually every kind of plant absorbs energy from the sun through photosynthesis. It's how they stay alive. Life's only possible because of this energy. With it, living things can produce new cells and flourish. Also, thanks to this energy, fruits and berries ripen and vegetables grow. Then animals, and us humans too, can feed on them. It's this, the same energy, that enables them to survive, mature, reproduce and live their brief lives. To put it simply, it enables everything to exist. But, for some reason I don't understand, people aren't using this energy. Honestly, how can people be so foolish, so ignorant?"

10

Güneş spoke: "You're right, Doğa. These days, people don't know how to make use of the sun. But it wasn't always like that. There were times when people used the sun much more than they do now. Long ago, people devised an incredible number of ways to make use of the sun's energy, and some of these we saw for ourselves and learned about while we were on Sun Mountain."

"But…" said Gök, hesitating, "What do you mean exactly? Are you saying that nowadays people aren't more advanced? Do you mean civilizations haven't really progressed and we aren't really living in a *modern* age?"

Güneş smiled patiently and said, "What you're saying is true, my friend, or rather people think it's true. But the fact is, the truth is actually very different."

"So," said Gök, "Are you telling us it *isn't* true, and civilization and culture *haven't* developed?"

"Well…" Güneş replied, "It really depends on how you look at it. You see, capitalism thrives by taking control of energy, just as it does with everything else. It's a system that exploits people by dominating the oil, coal and nuclear energy industries. In other words, people become dependent on them, and believe they can't manage without them and don't have any alternatives… If you like, they've become hooked on them. These days, most of us feel as if we've become slaves to the capitalist system and changing it is way too complicated. To put it another way, it isn't possible for us to use the extraordinary energy of the sun that shines over our heads, as we're already totally dependent on the energy systems created by capitalism."

Inspired by what Güneş had said, Su asked: "Would it ever be possible for us to get rid of this unfair system and develop

11

a new one that uses the sun?" Without a second thought, Güneş replied, "Of course we could... But only if we use our awareness of the Sun Philosophy that we learned on Sun Mountain. We've all seen how the sun was once used in Anatolian culture. The Wise Ones of the Sun have taught us all about it. What we've got to do now, and without delay, is to create the first actual Solar Village, starting with our own village. Gök agreed: "Yes, yes... you're right. I really believe we can do this; just as other people are. People who know about sun philosophy..."

Ay interrupted: "Hey! Not so fast, Gök... It won't be as easy as you imagine... People only think according to the prevailing system: what they already know. It's more than likely most people will reject the idea of solar projects. They might even try to stop us. Seriously, it's going to be hard, very hard; an uphill struggle." The others knew that what Ay had said was absolutely right, but even so they were all determined to put what they had learned into practice. Filled with determination, they continued on their way to the village.

A Reunion

Arriving at the village, the young companions were met with a profound silence. The whole place looked as if it were asleep. There was no one about: no adults, no children. What could have happened to them and why was everywhere so silent?

Walking along the lane, they encountered a young girl. They looked at her carefully from a distance but could find nothing out of the ordinary about her face. Nor did there appear to be anything unusual about the situation. She was simply smiling at them, as she did with everybody. Running towards them she cried, "You're here at last! Everybody's been so worried about you... Where have you been?"

A small, kind-hearted child of about twelve years old, Ayşe was always cheerful. She hugged them in a friendly way and kissed them one by one. It was only then that the youngsters became aware that something was wrong. Something about her embrace seemed different as if it embodied another sense or feeling. Her behaviour surprised the youngsters. What was she trying to tell them?

Everyone knew that the young companions had been away on a journey, so why should they be bothered about them? Ayşe kept pace with the group and as they continued, they were joined by other villagers. People started coming out of their houses and gardens to walk with them, so in the end, there was quite a crowd. Güneş and his friends began to get a strange sensation. What could all this mean? They'd never experienced anything like it. Something odd was going on, and they didn't understand what it was.

The young friends gave each other concerned glances, but none of them were any the wiser. Then they became aware of something that completely astonished them. They realised that they were being surrounded by children of all ages. Most were much younger than they were and were watching them, following in their wake without making a sound. By the time they reached the village square, the numbers had grown significantly. Something was clearly happening. As Güneş continued walking, he was mulling over the situation in his mind. It was certainly unexpected, but what could it be?

Customarily, guests were always welcomed at the entrance to the village and villagers would always try to help them in whatever way they could. But this kind of hospitality was for people who were coming to the village for the first time and of course, Güneş and his friends were not guests. As youngsters, they would often go climbing in the mountains and return to the village without any fuss or bother. Although Güneş was well aware of the old customs and traditions of the village, he also knew that it was the first time something like this had happened and it perplexed him.

Ayşe was walking next to Güneş and Ay couldn't resist whispering to her: "What's going on, Ayşe? Why are all these children joining us? Why are they walking with us?" "I don't think anything's wrong," Ayşe replied brightly, in her usual cheerful manner. "They're probably just inquisitive." Ay was surprised by her friend's quip and not knowing how to respond, remained silent.

According to Ayşe, there was nothing wrong or mysterious. They had simply been to the mountain and returned unharmed. So, why were children tagging along with them and behaving so curiously? What possible reason could there be for these children escorting Güneş and his friends?

As they continued on their way through the village, people started to open their windows. The people inside looked out and began to wave. Although the grownups weren't joining the crowd, they were greeting them, smiling cheerfully. It was as if they were saying "welcome," but no one came out of their houses to join the procession; they were simply waving and smiling. The situation was becoming even more intriguing. What was the matter? What could be going on?

Ay and Güneş were now at the head of the convoy.

Ayşe was behind them, followed by Su, Gök and Doğa. By now, about thirty children had joined them; all of them marching in complete silence. There was no sound apart from their footsteps. Gök was as baffled as the others. Doğa and Su continued to walk but were deep in thought. Su turned to her friend and murmured under her breath: "This is incredible, Doğa. I've never seen or heard of anything like this in my entire life."

Su's character was different. If truth be told, she had several traits that evoked her name, Water. Just like her namesake, she was sometimes very calm, but at other times she could be incredibly wild and spirited. She was intriguing, in that she could go anywhere, everywhere, no matter how difficult or impossible it appeared, or so it seemed to everyone else. Her temperament was such that nobody could stop her from doing exactly what she wanted. She adored roaming in the mountains and wandering through deep valleys and across plains. She also loved exploring dark caves. As a result, she was considered to be very perceptive but, on this occasion, even she wasn't clear about what was happening.

Now, Doğa, on the other hand, was much more affected than her companions. This was something she hadn't previously experienced and the village children's curious behaviour really troubled her. Doğa had a "giving" personality. Affectionate and compassionate, she loved everybody, but she could also be strong-willed and stubborn.

As her name–which means nature in Turkish–implied, she adored nature and used to do battle with anyone who damaged it or harmed wildlife. In other words, every feature of the natural world could be seen in her personality and people who knew her well were all deeply aware of her qualities. On one occasion, it was said of her, "Doğa [Nature] has become human and started to walk" and these words, spoken by an anthropologist who visited the village, will never be forgotten: "She isn't human. She's Cybele, come back to life."

Still feeling very puzzled by what was going on, the young companions – the Children of the Sun – continued towards the village square, followed by a crocodile of youngsters.

The Village Square

When at last they turned the final corner, they couldn't believe their eyes. There, standing before them   was something they really hadn't expected. A huge crowd filled the square. It appeared as if the entire village was waiting for them.

As Güneş and his friends entered the square, there was a huge burst of applause. They looked around, astonished by what they were seeing and hearing. Everyone they knew was there, clapping, cheering and beaming from ear to ear. As the companions hurried towards their families, tremendous excitement and a sense of overwhelming emotion filled the air. First of all, the young friends greeted and embraced their own parents, then they greeted everyone else.

While they were shaking hands, they were also thinking, "What's all this about, why's everybody here?"

It all felt very peculiar, but they weren't sure why. Only when the greetings had finally subsided, and silence returned did they learn what was going on. An old man with a white beard called Hancı Dede approached the group of friends, peering closely at them as he did so. "After you'd climbed the mountain," he said, in a clear, strong voice, but one tinged with emotion, "we heard that you were lost in the Dark Forest. This was when the village began to worry about you. Now, thank goodness, you've come home safe and sound, and are with us once again. We are truly overjoyed."

In less than no time, Hancı Dede, who everyone called White Beard, had explained what the villagers had been feeling. They had heard that the youngsters had become lost and were naturally extremely concerned. In a voice brimming with emotion, Güneş' mother said: "Somehow you managed to

17

get through the canyons and enter the forest. Nobody's ever been able to do that before..." Her feelings finally overcame her, and her voice cracked with pent up emotion... She cried: "You all vanished... you disappeared like puffs of smoke... We didn't hear any news about you... for ages." Full of a mother's tenderness, she again embraced her son in her strong, loving arms, as if she would never let him go. The young friends now began to realise just how frightened she must have been during that time.

As it happened, it had been the shepherd who had told the villagers about the disappearance of the young friends in the forest, and in the days that followed they had all waited for some good news. But there was nothing, not a word, and the parents who by now were thinking that they had lost their children forever, were in a state of high anxiety. Volunteers came forward to form a rescue team and although they had spent days and nights searching for the youngsters, all their efforts had been in vain.

As the villagers became less optimistic and more physically exhausted and emotionally drained, their unease increased and as more time passed without news, the more worried they became.

Finally, after no word was received about their loved ones' fate, everyone began to lose hope. Some began to say that they were sure the young friends had been killed or had died. Their despair increased until nearly all of the villagers started to believe that their young ones were lost forever. There were murmurings in the village, like "What a tragedy! They're too young to die! They were all *so* healthy and *so* beautiful!"

Of course, it goes without saying, those most affected by these rumours were the parents of the young companions. They had not been able to avoid hearing the gossip. Their fathers begged the mountain shepherds to look for them and they too took part in the search. Back at home, their mothers constantly prayed for good news and from time to time wept. It was a heart-breaking situation, as everybody was beginning to seriously believe that the young companions were dead.

Waves of profound sadness began to engulf the village with some villagers even visiting the families to offer their condolences. Despite this, the parents could never accept that their children were dead. They had always had faith in them and were certain that they would somehow be able to survive, whatever the circumstances. And in this they were correct. Even as the villagers continued to doubt and were gripped by a deep melancholy, it was lively young Ayşe who had first noticed the youngsters' return.

Stretched out on the balcony, she had been gazing at the Legend Mountain and thinking about her lost friends. Then, as if in a daydream, she caught a glimpse of them in the forest. To begin with, she was unable to believe what she was seeing. She looked at them carefully rubbing her eyes. No, it was definitely true. What she was looking at was real; the five young comrades were standing on the hill, looking at the village.

"Mum! Mum!" yelled Ayşe. Her voice was so agitated, her mother, Hatice came running, very concerned: "What's happened, Ayşe? What's all the fuss about?" "I've seen them, mum! They're alive." Ayşe was breathless with excitement. Curious, Hatice looked at where Ayşe was pointing. Although she scanned the forest carefully, she could see nothing. She thought her daughter must have been dreaming, but Ayşe insisted: "Look, look... there, on that small hill, over there in the forest!"

Again, Hatice looked again and this time she was able to see the young companions standing on a grassy slope. "Yes, yes. I can see now," she cried. "It's them!" Hatice loved this young group of friends and always spoke of them with admiration. She would say: "One day they will come back to enlighten us." She was really distressed when they were thought to have been lost. But now, all of them were there, alive, right in front of her. She couldn't believe her eyes. Turning to Ayşe, she said: "Go, go, my child. Run to the square and tell everyone this wonderful news."

Ayşe sprinted down the stairs as fast as she could. Opening the gate, she immediately turned towards the square. She was determined to share this good news with everybody. Once there, she began to yell: "They're alive! they're alive!"

A small group of children were in the square. Like the rest of the village, they were miserable; talking about their missing friends and sharing memories of them. With Ayşe's shouts, they fell silent, looking around to see where the voice was coming from. "Yes, yes... They're... They're all alive," panted Ayşe, completely out of breath. "I promise... I swear to you... I've seen them." The children's eyes widened, and their mouths opened with amazement. Ayşe repeated again and again that their friends, who were thought to be dead, were in fact still alive. First, they couldn't believe their ears. Then Ayşe pointed at the hill: "Look, Look! Here they are... They're coming now," she announced.

The children watched as their friends approached; the self-same friends they thought had been lost forever, in the forest. Without waiting a moment longer, they all hurried home to tell their families the good news.

As the news about the youngsters' return spread, joy began to replace the sadness and sense of hopelessness that had gripped the village for the previous ten days. As the villagers heard what was happening, they began to gather in the square, expressing their gratitude to Ayşe for bringing them such wonderful tidings. As they waited, one of the elders called Ayşe over to him and said: "Come on then! Go and welcome them home!"

Ayşe raced across the square, catching up with the group as they strode through the village.

Until now, Güneş had not been aware of what was happening. He only understood the villagers' feelings as he entered the square and saw the villagers, their families, and friends all waiting for them, and their enthusiast welcome.

If truth be told, this kind of feeling is not so unusual for those who are familiar with village life and customs. Communities like these have existed for thousands of years, and they know how to share feelings with each other that are painful, sweet and sad, as well as compassionate and awesome. For this reason, the village had developed some very important qualities that are rarely seen elsewhere. Values, such as sharing and solidarity, were highly regarded and resulted in their having an incredible level of compassion, as well as their being ready to accept the resurgence of the Anatolian Sun Culture.

The First Meeting

When the young companions met everyone in the village square, they were deeply moved and their attitudes towards them utterly changed. They began to love and respect them. The sadness of the whole village, followed by the enthusiastic welcome, touched them deeply. At first, they were uncertain what to do but then they realized what the villagers were expecting of them. The villagers were wondering what had happened and how Güneş and his friends had become lost.

Also, they were curious to learn how had they managed to enter, let alone survive, the Dark Forest. Surely it was a place in which nobody could survive. Hadn't some villagers even said that such a thing was nigh on impossible? For them to survive must have been nothing short of a miracle. There were so many questions in the villagers' minds, and they were eager to learn the facts. Having been really distressed by what had happened, they were now ready to listen. So, everyone waited patiently in the square, to hear what the youngsters had to say for themselves.

By now, Güneş and his friends were all too aware of these expectations. They sat on a platform in a corner of the square, all set to tell the villagers about their journey. The square was hushed, the audience tense with anticipation. Güneş began to speak: "On behalf of our group, I want to thank you all; first, for your concern and then for welcoming us so warmly. We're quite overwhelmed. We think of ourselves as being a part of you. Essentially, we're all the same – not so different. We are like members of one big family and because of this, our feelings are incredibly strong for each other. Once again, many thanks.

Rising to speak, Gök adopted the same conciliatory manner: "You're absolutely right Güneş. We appreciate that you've all been desperately worried about us and we want to say sorry for making you feel like that. Basically, we got lost in the Dark Forest and for a while, we didn't know what to do or where to go. The forest was so completely and utterly dark, we felt engulfed by it." Now, everybody was listening with bated breath. The suspense was almost palpable. In a wave of collective empathy, the villagers were finally able to sense the fear the young people must have felt when they became lost in the forest.

Su continued: "Can you imagine what it was like for us? We were totally lost. We could hear the sounds of wild animals as they got nearer and nearer. To be honest, we were terrified and there were moments when we thought we were going to die."

As the young comrades continued with their story, the same sensations of fear and dread they had experienced spread through the crowd. The villagers now began to understand how the youngsters must have felt too. But even so, the question that remained foremost in everyone's minds was, "Why didn't you tell us?"

Doğa, who until then had been sitting quietly in the corner, rose to speak: "Just as we were facing total despair, something really miraculous happened. We caught a glimpse of a faint glow of light in the distance and it was this that eventually saved us; helping us to overcome our fears and regain hope. We began to move towards this light. Yes, this light, which helped us to hold on to life and stay alive, was the Light of the Sun and yet it came from the depths of a cave.

"Ohhh…" This was the sound of the crowd exhaling deeply. It was only when they heard the word 'light' that everybody could finally breathe a sigh of relief. The miracle had been a light and it was this light that had saved the youngsters…

Unlike modern, urban communities, these villagers were deeply aware of the importance of light. In other words, they knew how vital light is for humanity. The word has a powerful association for village cultures and once the villagers had heard it, they understood and were able to relax. Ay studied the faces in the crowd and murmured softly as if to herself, "What *beautiful* people you are!"

With her affectionate gaze, it seemed as if she were holding the crowd in a warm embrace. The intensity of Ay's reaction affected everybody and created a unique moment of tenderness. It was something quite extraordinary. The intensity of their mutual affection had made them as one; like a single soul, in a single body.

As Ay observed the crowd, she remembered a saying from her forebears: "Humans are one entity and what unites them is their love for one another." She desperately wanted to say something, but she couldn't find the right words, so she decided to keep quiet. Then, quite suddenly and unexpectedly, as much as to herself as to everyone else, she exclaimed: "We love you all *so* much!" These simple but intensely emotional words brought the villagers back to reality. Yes! Ay had managed to condense all their thoughts and feelings in a way that was worthy of the Love of God.

A hush descended on the crowd again. Every person there now understood how and why the young friends had become lost, and their despair and fear vanished, to be replaced by joy and love. The youngsters' fatigue was clear for all to see and with these words, Güneş brought the meeting to a close: "We have encountered many obstacles and faced many dangers. We've also discovered new things about humanity, which we shall certainly be sharing with you. If it's ok with you, we'd like to get together again in a day or so to discuss them. As you now know, we have been on a long and sometimes very scary and dangerous journey and we are all absolutely exhausted. So, for now, please let us rest."

Quietly, slowly the companions walked away from the gathering and headed to their respective homes, where they fell fast asleep as soon as their heads hit their pillows.

Talks

Inevitably, the disappearance and sudden reappearance of the young comrades became the only topic of conversation. Quite literally, everybody was talking about what had happened. When people met each other in the street or market, they spoke about it and of course it goes without saying, everyone had *something to say*. The subject of the most speculation was what Güneş had said. "We have discovered new things about humanity, which we shall certainly be sharing with you."

The villagers had already started to ask about and comment on his words: "What could the discoveries be?" Both young and old were asking the same question. "What had Güneş meant? What could there possibly be on the mountain? What did they discover?" One of the younger villagers remarked, "Perhaps Güneş said it just for fun," while another ventured: "He might have said it just to make us wonder." Yet another dismissed these remarks, saying, "I know Güneş. He's not someone who makes idle talk."

Despite all the villagers' deliberations about what had happened, they were unable to find any answers. It seemed so impossible. The sages and the elders of the village pondered at length over what young Güneş had said, but even they couldn't agree. One speculated, "I think they might really have experienced and learned new things." Another said more pessimistically, "They're still young and lacking experience. They could be embroidering what they've seen." But what they were all really wondering was what the young friends had seen, lived through, endured and learned   .

For the most part, it was the children who were really curious about what had happened. They had been very startled by their brothers' and sisters' disappearance and sudden reappearance and they listened to what was being said about them as if it was a story. At the same time, they were also wondering what the next chapter would be.

The village women had gathered in one of their homes, where they were discussing the young companions' strange experiences. They had some different ideas about what could have happened but mostly they discussed how they were able to survive. One young woman wondered out loud, "What on earth did they eat and how were they able to find food?" This question was rather sensible, as it's not at all easy to find food and water in the Dark Forest. Another woman's question, on the other hand, was rather more inquisitive, verging on prying: "I wonder if they developed any emotional feelings for each other or have fallen in love?" The woman who asked this question was well known for being the local chinwag.

She would often watch people furtively, trying to figure out with whom they would most likely fall in love. Most kept away from this woman, Fatma, but even so, whenever they met with her alone, they would sidle up to her to ask things like, "What's the latest on so-and-so?" Some of them would, on the face of it, appear not to be interested, saying, "Why are you so nosy? It's just an ordinary story. We've heard loads of tales like this, and this is just one them." But despite their outward lack of interest, they were actually just as inquisitive as she was to learn what had happened. Questions and explanations flourished; from the eldest to the youngest, everybody was gossiping and searching for answers.

But nobody understood what Güneş had meant and nobody had any idea about what the young friends had discovered. The more time that passed, the more their sense of wonder and curiosity increased. It was essential to discuss all this but first, everyone needed to sleep. The following day an announcement was made over the village's loudspeaker system to say that the youngsters were rested, and everyone would meet up by the big fire at 8 pm.

Everybody in the village was delighted to hear this. Finally, all their questions and speculations would be answered. As the hour of the meeting approached, they began to grow impatient. As darkness fell, a group of young people arrived in the square and began to gather wood to build a fire. As the flames took hold, the sky lit up and the blaze could be seen far and wide. Everybody was able to see the fire from their homes and they began to head towards it, almost as if they had been hypnotised.

For the villagers, the fire was held to be as sacred as the sun, and sun culture had a history in the village that had endured for a thousand years. The villagers used to sing folk songs about fire and tell stories about it too. There also used to be enactments, a sort of theatre, relating to the fire at wedding ceremonies and bayrams (religious festivals). There had long been a fire pit in the centre of the square, which had been around for so long, no one could remember how it came to be there.

A work of art in itself, it was a huge granite boulder, the centre of which had been carved out to form a hollow. Six bronze rods encircling the pit rose to a point at its centre. In the middle of each rod there was a sphere and a larger globe, also made of bronze, was suspended from the apex. These seven spheres shone brilliantly. It was understood that this fire pit symbolized the sky, the planets, and the sun. Held to be the most important creation in the village, everyone who saw it found it captivating.

By now it was almost eight o'clock. The leaping flames from this sacred fire were illuminating the square in every direction. Even though it was well past sunset, the fire continued to fill the square with light, as though it were the sun. By the time Güneş and his friends came to the square, the villagers had already arrived and taken their seats. Brimming with anticipation, the crowd was becoming increasingly excited but even so, perfect silence fell as the young companions climbed onto a raised platform and took their seats.

The head of the village, Muhtar Bayındır, was the first to speak: "For the last ten days we've all been through some pretty incredible events. First, we lost our children and were overcome with grief. Then we found them and were over the moon. These events have reminded us just how much we love each other and what happened has united us all in a state of intense emotion. Grief and elation, in turn,　have brought our entire village together, as one. I hope you'll remember this spirit of unity whenever we're in trouble, as it will make us stronger in every possible way.

"I want to thank these bright and plucky young people. They've passed this challenging task – a kind of coming of age – a baptism of fire if you like – most admirably. Today, they are standing before us with their fully-fledged adult personalities and we're now looking forward to them making many useful contributions to our village. Meanwhile, we're all fascinated to learn about their extraordinary adventures. We can't wait to find out what they've learned　on our sacred mountain and what momentous things they're planning for us."

Having summed up the villagers' thoughts and feelings, the Muhtar left the stage to Güneş and his friends.

Following a good night's sleep, the youngsters were looking completely refreshed. Their tiredness had gone, and a nervous energy had taken its place. They looked self-assured and were raring to go. From this time onwards they would become known as the Children of the Sun but first, they had to find a way to explain their extraordinary experiences...

Chapter 2

The Sun Declaration

A letter from Grandfather Sun

Taking a deep breath as he rose to his feet, Güneş scanned the crowd and saw hundreds of pairs of eyes shining brightly in the firelight, looking back at him and his friends. He was so overwhelmed by what he saw that for a moment he didn't know quite what to say. Then his gaze was drawn to the flames of the fire pit and the sphere representing the sun shining above them. For an instant he thought about the Sun Mountain, remembering the mysterious adventures they had so recently experienced. At that moment, quite suddenly, Güneş raised his voice: "We have..." he said, faltering slightly with emotion, "We have seen the Mysterious Garden of the Sun."

These words hit the villagers like a bombshell. They thought about the Sun Legend, a story inherited from their ancestors. But everyone had been told it was a myth. Could this story about the Mysterious Garden, the one described in the legend, be true after all? They couldn't believe their ears. Su understood the mood: "It's true!" she exclaimed. "It's the same light we saw when we got lost in the forest. Honestly, the light coming from the Sun Garden is the light of the sun. We were able to get there by following the light we'd seen in those dark winding caves. We were astonished by the magnificence of what we saw but simply never imagined that there could be such a beautiful and mysterious garden."

One by one, the young friends described what they had seen and experienced in the Mysterious Garden[1]. The stories they told were not so different from the tales they had already heard but this time these were not myths. The villagers were deeply affected and not a little confused by what they were hearing. It was now Doğa's turn to speak: "Actually, the Garden of the Sun is a miniature version of the nature that surrounds our own world. Nearly everything we see in nature can also be found there. But unlike here, there's no pollution, no wrack, and ruin. It teaches us how nature should be and how we could sustain and protect it."

Gök spoke next: "What really astounded us though, was our meeting with the Wise Ones of the Sun." These words only increased the villagers' bewilderment and confusion. Although they had heard of scholars, such as biologists and ecologists, it was the first time they had heard of the Wise Ones of the Sun. They turned to each other as if to ask, "Who are they?" How could Güneş possibly explain the Wise Ones of the Sun? He paused to think for an instant, before continuing: "The Wise Ones of the Sun are the sages who lead and encourage the development of the Sun Culture. They showed us how life began on earth with the sun's rays, solar energy, and how it has altered, advanced and still continues."

An older man in the crowd exclaimed: "Are you telling us that all the stories we've been told about creation and how life exists on earth are wrong?" Güneş knew that how he replied would be critical. How could they explain that all the myths, legends and stories, which have been told and etched unquestioningly in people's minds for thousands of years,

---

[1] *Read about the young companions' adventures on Sun Mountain in my book: "The Mysterious Garden of the Sun". 2016, Ankara*

were wrong? But he also knew that they should be aware of the reality.

"I can't really comment on what fairy tales and stories you believe in," he continued. "But life on earth originally came about and developed because of the sun's energy and its power. The Wise Ones of the Sun explained all this to us scientifically and told us that any theories and beliefs that ignore this will never take us down the right path."

A villager remarked: "I understand what you're saying... but what do you mean by 'the right path'? Are you saying we're on the wrong path? If so, what wrong things are we doing?" Gök replied: "Well, we already know more or less that something is definitely going wrong. For example, you are probably already aware that the weather in our village is becoming warmer. There's less rain than there used to be and for the first time, we're beginning to have droughts. Some of the springs have dried up and there are streams that aren't flowing anymore. The balance of our climate has changed. Also, due to late frosts, some of our earlier crops have frozen and gone to waste. As a consequence of all this, our village is suffering."

Everyone nodded. They understood and were already aware of climate change in the village and the various catastrophes that were devastating their farming. Su added: "We're all seeing and experiencing this, aren't we? What's happening in the rest of the world is also happening here in our village too. Haven't we polluted our water and soil by using chemicals and detergents? Don't we also eat crops that we've grown in manmade compost and toxic chemicals? Haven't we begun to use fossil fuels - coal and petrol - instead of traditional kinds of energy, such as biofuel, the sun, wood, plants, and animal waste? Hasn't our air been polluted? Ha-

33

ven't illnesses and premature deaths increased? Isn't our water and soil polluted? Everywhere is full of rubbish and waste. Our village used to be a paradise. Are we still able to say that today?"

Even though most of the villagers already knew about the things Su was saying, her words aroused the listeners. A cry of "Yes! Yes! Yes!" had begun to echo among her listeners. All the villagers had been affected by these concerns and were secretly upset by them. But the words they were hearing changed their gloom into a call for action. Nerves were tense. It was as if their fate was no longer inevitable. This time, it was a decisive "No, no, no" that echoed around the square. Doğa spoke up: "This thing called 'modern civilization' is no longer either modern or civilised. It has become the enemy of nature. This so-called civilization regularly pollutes the environment and the natural world, destroying biodiversity; damaging life itself. It's time to do away with this so-called 'modern civilization' that exploits nature."

How could it be called *civilization* if it destroys nature? The villagers felt that the words Doğa used were harsh, but they also knew that what she was saying was the present-day reality. When they started to think about global deforestation and the extinction of plant and animal species, they knew that they had to agree with her.

It was Su who took the debate to the next level. "Not only do these things damage nature," she said, "they also exploit people. Just a few families and countries have total control over the whole system. They have been using and exploiting the rest of the world – countries as well as people – for their own ends. Hunger is widespread; thousands of people are dying each year because of hunger. Respect for humanity has almost disappeared and any feelings of solidarity and sharing are vanishing. There's now a new lifestyle; one based on money and personal desires. Love, the most valuable and sacred emotion in our lives, is no longer present. Is it possible to call such a system, one where a small minority exploits the world, "civilization"?

Ay could not hold back her feelings a moment longer: "In my opinion" she announced," this *thing* we call "modern civilization" is a system based on outcomes rather than love. We've started to live in a loveless world. Destructive feelings grow rapidly when there is no love; the numbers of wars and conflicts increase and as a result, the world is becoming increasingly impossible to live in. We can see for ourselves that behind all the wars and conflicts in today's world, which are killing hundreds of thousands of people, there is a loveless civilization based on nothing more than greed and exploitation."

With Ay's words, everybody turned to look at each other, wide-eyed. Everything she said was true. Unfortunately, the rapidly expanding and exploitative capitalist system that was spreading throughout the world had also impacted on their village; feelings of love in the village has gradually decreased, despite their customs and traditions that continued from the past. Instead, tension and quarrels had begun to take their place. This development was disturbing and everyone in the village was concerned. It was as if Ay had read their minds.

One of the more impoverished villagers, who until that moment had been sitting quietly in a corner, intervened: "You've explained our experiences very well. But I'm wondering what the association between these negative developments, the sun, Sun Culture and so on, actually is? To be honest, that's something we still don't understand." Güneş very much appreciated the villager's astute question. He was absolutely right. While they had been talking about the events

35

that had taken place in the mountain, the topic of their conversation had shifted.

The world's problems definitely influenced the village too. The village community, as well as the countryside that surrounded it, in which life had continued peacefully for thousands of years, had certainly been negatively affected. But what was the relationship between them, the sun and its culture?

It was, therefore, Güneş who was first to reply: "Thank you. The answer to your question is directly connected with our journey to the mountain and what we learned there. While on the Sun Mountain, we saw the solutions we need to solve the problems we are experiencing here. We not only saw what needs to be done, we came across some examples too and there's also what the Wise Ones of the Sun told us. What's more, as I told you yesterday, we have discovered new things relating to humanity, which I said I would definitely share with you. So, if it's alright with you, we would now like to read the declaration given to us by the Wise Ones of the Sun."

Before he could continue, Bayındır, the village Muhtar, intervened: "You have brought us good news and a salutation from Sun Mountain. You have also explained our village's problems very clearly and for all this we thank you. We must discuss this together and try to find solutions. But first, like everyone here today, I would like to hear the Sun Declaration. So, let's all listen to the message from the mountain!"

A cry rose up from the crowd, "Yes! Yes, we want to hear it too!" In her hand, Su held the declaration she had been given by Grandfather Sun, one of the Wise Ones of the Sun. She began to read fluently, like water.

Dear young friends,

With people waging war for their own gain, the situation in the world is becoming worse, day by day. These situations will either exploit or destroy everyone.

Some countries are ruthlessly committing these acts of violence in a more organized way. Millions of people are hungry, migrating, dying or being killed. There must be an end to this violence and brutality so that life and social order can return. There has to be a new existence, one based on respect and love.

Humanity has unwittingly used up all nature's resources. The toxic chemicals they use are damaging nature; every living thing is being poisoned. They're meddling with the very essence of their being, what makes them what they are, destroying their naturalness in the process.

It is high time these dangerous developments were brought to an end. As the young generation, you must step up to the mark; become active. Your first responsibility will be to save mankind from the pit of darkness and ignorance.

You must tell them about the realities of life. They must learn that they are part of the energy system, not separate from it. They must never forget that they exist only because of sunlight, and it is this light, sent by the sun, that keeps them alive.

My dear young friends, never forget, today's social system is a tarnished civilization in every way and the time has come for mankind to be rid of it   . You must start working on a civilization that is sustainable for both the natural world and humanity.

This new civilization must be in harmony with sunlight and its energy. A system that is compatible with life forces does not harm either nature or mankind. Quite the reverse, they support and enhance each other.

The civilization that we need to develop is called the Sun Civilization.

The Sun Civilization will bestow light on you and show you the right path.

First of all, it is essential that you get rid of the fossil fuel waste that is polluting the atmosphere and environment. Instead, you should use Solar energy and its spin-offs.

Towns, cities, and industries that operate using these energies must be established. In addition, you must develop new technologies that employ these energies. The most ideal living environments are villages, towns and cities powered by solar energy. Of course, this means that solar technology and architecture has to be developed across all areas.

My dear young people do not forget, the future of life on earth rests in your hands. The Civilization of Light that you will establish will shine like a sun in the skies of the future."

These words of Grandfather Sun were like a ray of light in the darkness! There were no longer any pessimists among the listeners; instead, their minds were full of insight. Now they knew what to do and how to do it. With this new realisation, the crowd rose from their seats as one and applauded the young companions for what seemed like ages.

The meeting was over, and the villagers returned to their homes. Everyone was full of new and creative feelings and thoughts and their hearts were filled with hope. It was as if they were flying, soaring.

Children of the Sun

The following day, the village elders gathered first thing. Having considered what the young companions had gone through on the mountain and what they later described in the village square, the council agreed that they were sufficiently mature and experienced to be asked to take their places as adult members of the village.

After telling the youngsters about their decisions, they announced it to the villagers. The five young comrades, Güneş, Gök, Doğa, Ay, and Su, were now considered to be grown up but, as yet, they were only candidates. According to village tradition, there would have to be a coming of age ceremony. They would also be given new titles and the participants who took part in this had to approve these decisions. All the villagers had to be there too.

Everyone was notified that the ceremony would be held that night. All the arrangements were made, according to village tradition. *Saz* and *davul* players were invited. Tables were set up in the middle of the square. The fire pit was refreshed. The preparations, which continued all day, were finally completed towards the evening.

Dusk was accompanied by a momentous calm throughout the village. Suddenly, front doors opened and almost the entire community, men women and children, began to walk in the same direction, towards the fire. They were laughing cheerfully. Villagers were pouring into the square; many with baskets in their hands. Nearly everyone had prepared some traditional dishes and had brought drinks with them.

As they arrived at the square, before taking their seats they placed the food and drink they'd bought with them on the tables. As young Ayşe appeared and approached the platform

39

there was a discernible hush. She announced the programme. First, she said, there would be the ceremony and then the feasting would begin. At last, they could all have fun together. The village Muhtar, Bayındır, stood up to greet everybody.

"You all know why we are here," he announced. "We want to receive these five young people, who went to the mountain and got lost but then returned safely – thank goodness – as adult members of our community. Before we proceed, is there anybody who would like to speak, or who objects to this decision?

There was a brief silence, during which no one said a word. After all, these young people had gained everyone's respect and established their authority in the villagers' hearts. Everybody looked as if they approved the decision, so the Muhtar continued: "It is accepted. Well done", he said, adding, "We give them this title: The Children of the Sun. Considering the wisdom they have brought us, it is a title that they thoroughly deserve."

When Muhtar Bayındır concluded his speech, there was a standing ovation. As the clapping eventually died down, Ayşe stood and walking towards   the spectators, she took Ayben by the hand. Walking onto the stage together, Ayben took her seat and picked up her saz, while Ayşe announced: "Now it's time to feast, but just before we do, we're going to listen to Ayben; who, as you know, is a wonderful musician. Let's see if you all like the new song that she's composed for us tonight."

The crowd remained silent as they waited for Ayben, one of the village's favourite performers, to begin. Unhurriedly, her clear, mellow voice filled the night air. How beautifully she sang! Everybody held their breath. The words of the song were so full of meaning and marvelous messages.

Children of the sun

You overwhelmed us with grief
Then you brought us joy
Walking in the dark forests without fear
You went to the summit of the mountain
How beautiful you are!
I've fallen in love with you all
Your hearts are tender
Your eyes shine like fire
You know no fear
What beautiful youngsters you are!
Tigers and lions are your brothers
Wolves and rabbits are your comrades
Fish and crocodiles are your friends
Accompanied by birds of paradise
You walked towards the sun
What beautiful friends you are!
No one loves nature more than you
The rivers, the seas, and the earth
The sky is your love garden
The sun, the stars, and the moon are your lovers
Your world is shining bright
What beautiful comrades you are!

Ayben's soulful and expressive voice spread like an invisible wave through the crowd, touching everybody's hearts. Now the young people were their children too, and they realised that they would be walking with them towards a bright future. As Ayben finished her enchanting song, everyone began to tuck into the food. Afterwards, they listened to more songs about nature, the sun and of course, love.

Accompanied by *davul* and *zurna* the music continued long into the night. As the sunrise proclaimed the start of a new day there also came new understanding and new hope. It was a long time since the villagers had been so happy…

The Picnic

It had been a long, exciting and exhausting night, so everyone slept until late. However, when they did awake, they were smiling. With new hope filling their hearts, the pessimism had gone, and it seemed as if the troubled days were finally behind them.

The message from Grandfather Sun had not only made it clear that they were not alone, it had also given them the advice they needed to start establishing a bright new world. This message was so much more than the usual kind of speech they were used to hearing; it was a declaration, a guide, which would enlighten and lead them.

It was Sunday and although they had their regular chores to do, like feeding the animals, collecting the eggs and milking the cows, nobody really wanted to work. So, once these tasks were done, preparations were made for a picnic. Groups of villagers began to head towards the mountain and the forest.

The village was surrounded by rivers and springs; water flowed everywhere. The groups came together on the bank of a stream and spread colourful kilims, woven in the village of course, on the grass. Barbecues were lit, while the little ones played, and the elders chatted. The topic of conversation was the same in almost every group: the recent events. Even so, despite the topic being the same, the comments themselves varied. The subject of the conversation was the Wise Ones of the Sun and the general mood was cheerful.

One of the younger people present, enquired, "We haven't heard about the Wise Ones of the Sun before, where do they come from?" A middle-aged man joined the discussion. "It would appear," he said, "that some of you aren't aware of the Sun Legend. It says that it was the Wise Ones of the Sun who established and spread the Sun Culture." "Yes," remarked someone else. "I've heard that too. I've also heard that they're the ones who help people, sometimes whole societies, that are in crisis. They come and help by showing them the correct way."

"That's right," said another. "They're the ones who help groups of people or communities that are in trouble. According to the legend, these Wise Ones who live in the mountains, travel across the world to help build Sun Civilizations." "What Sun Civilizations?" Asked someone else. His friend responded directly: "There are legends about Sun Civilizations like the Inka, the Aztecs, the Egyptians and the Maya for example."

There was somebody else who had been keeping quiet, although he'd been attentively listening to the conversation. Nobody who knew his name but, as he knew a great deal, the villagers called him the Historian. Now the Historian joined the conversation. "It's true," he said. "As far as history is concerned, the Sun Civilizations were societies who reached the peak of civilisation. There have been Sun civilizations all over the world and although little has been written about it, one of the most advanced was the Anatolian Sun Civilisation. The most recent research carried out in Turkey has shown this to be the case."

Their discussions, which had begun with the mention of legends, had now moved onto actual civilizations. For many, it was the first time they had the term, "Anatolian Sun Civilization."

The Historian, who was, in fact, Emin Bey, a retired history teacher, spoke again: "The most recent archaeological studies in Anatolia have shown that this area was once the centre of the known world's civilization. This research suggests that

44

the building of the first house, the first temple, village, and city, all took place in Anatolia and that these very important concepts of architecture and town-planning began in Anatolia and spread to the rest of the world.

What Emin Bey said made a deep impression on his listeners. People came from other groups to join the discussion, which was becoming more and more animated. Then the old man, Hancı Dede, who the villagers knew as White Beard, and who had so far not broken his silence, began to speak. he could see that everyone was getting rather confused: "Unlike the other stories," he explained, "the Sun Legend isn't a myth. It's a true story that speaks of real life."

Mutters came from the crowd: "What? How can that be? Are you saying that what we were told before was wrong?" "No," responded Hancı Dede patiently. "There's no misunderstanding. Every society develops legends to be reminded of their origins, they all create myths about their own history. But these stories told in the past were anonymous and as a result, they have become what we call myths. But the Sun Legend is based on the realities of life and for this reason, it's different from the others."

Now everyone was totally confused. Could beliefs and scientific evidence be somehow combined? They asked him: "You're saying that the Sun Legend is true, aren't you? "Yes, I am. In fact, if you think about life and our planet, you can see that everything is associated with the sun. Everything you eat and drink for example. Plants, wherever they grow in the world, do so because of the sun. Fruit and vegetables develop and ripen thanks to the sun. And animals benefit from the sun's energy, too."

"But in the legend, the sun is said to be a god. Is there a Sun God?" White Beard replied without a moment's hesitation:

"Every legend contains elements of fact and each fact contains a legend. We should never forget that for as long as humanity has had the capacity to think, they have also been searching for the God that created them. Life on earth is related to the sun; so, in other words, sun meant God. For millions of years, people believed this and used to worship the sun. Then other gods and belief systems came along. These days, it isn't necessary for us to refer to the sun as "God." The sun itself is the source of life and, as life has no other source, there is no need for any other recognition."

The villagers only partly understood what Hancı Dede was saying. Yes, the Sun Legend was true but even so, there were some other, as yet unknown things, which they were waiting to be answered. "Well then, are the Sun's Priests described in the legend real?" "Yes, they are, just like we're real. In the past, these people were called the Wise Ones of the Sun. Now, we call them *solar scientists*. These are the people who know everything about the sun, about life and the relationship between life and nature. In the past, the information we gathered was passed from person to person. Nowadays, although small in number, there are still a few wise ones, who have this ancient knowledge of the sun."

Now, they finally understood and accepted everything they'd been told. But a final question was asked by an unexpectedly frail looking individual, who so far had said nothing: "So, what do you think about the Declaration from Grandfather Sun that our young friend read to us last night?"

Hancı Dede thought carefully about this question and did not reply immediately. He knew he should not say anything that could damage his listeners' self-confidence or affect the positive atmosphere that had been created so far. At the same time, he had to tell the truth. He turned towards the crowd and as he spoke, he looked intently into everyone's eyes: "In

46

my opinion, the Wise Ones thought it was time to act, so they sent the Declaration to us. In fact, they have clearly shown us what needs to be done. They are expecting us to put the sun project into practice. I hope we can, and, thanks to this project, we will have the opportunity to change our village."

"But will we really be able to put these projects into practice?" someone interjected.

"I think our village is very suitable, as it is one of the few villages in Anatolia that has lived with the sun culture and traditions for thousands of years. We can revive our traditions and develop projects using new techniques. Don't ever forget, the Wise Ones of the Sun chose our village and have prepared our young friends for the tasks ahead. Ultimately, they have sent them back to help us and, in this regard, we're very blessed."

Emin Bey and White Beard's clear explanations restored the villagers' hope. They were now filled with fresh enthusiasm. Elated by what had happened, they immediately tucked into their picnic. Then they all sang their new folk song, the Children of the Sun, and played games.

A productive meeting

Events in the village were making headway incredibly quickly. The village community council summoned the youngsters. They also invited some people of rank. They wanted to speak with the Children of the Sun to discover what they were planning to do.

It was Muhtar Bayındır who opened the discussion. "Each of you is a hero. This isn't just our opinion, it's everyone's. You are now among the most respected people in the village, but we would like to clarify the situation and learn what you think and what you would like to do. Basically, we want to help you as much as possible."

If truth be told, these words left the young friends feeling rather astonished. Everything was happening so fast. They were no longer just ordinary villagers. They were now considered to be mature and sensible adults; what's more, they were being called heroes. While they loved their village very much, many other young people had left the village and moved to the city. As a result, the number of young people living in the village was declining.

What's more, unemployment was increasing and becoming a serious problem. Poverty was becoming widespread too. Many young people who went to the city weren't happy with their living conditions and ended up in jobs they didn't like. In short, they were living in hardship.

Also, just as it was in other Anatolian villages, the gardens and fields were not being properly maintained and productivity was decreasing year by year.

The most important sources of income for the village appeared to be drying up. And, as if all this wasn't enough, local people were flocking to buy products that were sold in cities. In the past, villagers used to produce their own necessities and grow their own crops. But now they had become hooked on the urban lifestyle, which meant they could no longer meet their own needs, and these opportunistic systems were overwhelming the village. They couldn't even make their own bread.

The traditional and natural infrastructure of the village was also in the process of being destroyed. Artificial fertilizers and toxic chemicals had damaged the dignity of the village and polluted the environment. All the inhabitants felt deeply ill at ease and unhappy as a result of these problems. Was it only this village that suffered from these difficulties? Sadly not. Thousands of Anatolian villages shared the same destiny.

Anatolia's rich culture was in serious danger of obliteration. Ten thousand years of rich culture and history and millions of years of nature, in other words, the complex model of village life, was in the process of being annihilated; while, on the whole, villagers remained poor, hopeless and miserable.

On the other hand, the Children of the Sun were very clever and talented. All university graduates, they had found good jobs. Should they wish, they could choose to live and work overseas; anything was possible. But they had a different way of thinking. They had decided to stay in their village and do something for the local community. It was Güneş who answered the Muhtar's question: "As a group, we'd all to stay here and do good things for our village."

This answer perplexed the villagers. According to them, they, like their friends before them, would move away from their village and leave the local people to their destiny. All the same, it did not take long for them to grasp what was being said, leaving them with a great sense of satisfaction, instead. Their faces were now beaming with joy.

"I can't tell you how happy your decision has made us. Thank you so, so much," said Bayındır. "So, tell us, what is it that you'd like to do? How can we help you?" Gök was able to answer these questions on behalf of the entire group: "We don't want *you* to do anything, but if there's something you'd like us to do, then we want to do it too." During their long lives, the elders had seen and lived through many events.

For them, amazement was not something they felt, easily or often. Yet, somehow these young people kept on amazing them. One of the elders spoke up: "You're saying you'd like to do something for your village, aren't you?" Another old man joined in: "Our village needs so many things. We don't have a place, a guesthouse, where visitors can stay. We don't have a library or a community centre. Just one of these would be great. Which one would you like to do?"

In reality, there was a long list of things that the village lacked, and it wasn't possible for his question to be answered immediately. All these suggestions needed to be discussed and besides, whatever project they eventually chose, it would have to be one that was feasible. From now on, young friends would have to be totally reliable: when they promised to do something, they would have to fulfil it. Breaking a promise would never be an option.

It was Ay who replied: "As you know, we only left the village for the sake of our education, but we've been away for a long time. Now we'd like to learn in more detail the issues that the village has been facing. So, we can find the best way to proceed, we'll need to speak with everyone who lives here and learn their thoughts. Then we can share our findings with you

50

and finally, working together, we can decide how best to carry them out."

Everyone agreed with Ay's suggestion and the council was happy with the result. It would be necessary for any plan to be jointly evaluated but these young people were certainly well educated and could contribute new ideas; their words, opinions, and behaviour was proof of this.

Bayındır spoke again, on behalf of the council: "Well then, you are all most welcome. We're fascinated by your ideas and look forward to hearing the outcomes. We're now able to grant you full authority to carry out these village projects."

He looked at his fellow members on the council of elders for their approval, and everyone nodded to show their consent. Then they penned a document announcing their decision, which they all signed, and a copy was given to the youngsters. The original one was placed in an appropriate place in the village for everyone to see. It said:

An announcement to all villagers

Our young comrades, who are known as the Children of the Sun, have our authority to conduct a research project, to identify our village's problems and help with the development of the village. We request that everyone helps them in whatever way they need.

Signed by: The Village Council of Elders

The village council was a good one. Everyone involved had placed their trust in the youngsters and had given them much more power than the youngsters themselves or any other villager had anticipated. The young people were also aware of their responsibilities. In short, everyone at the meeting was pleased with the result because all the doors had been opened for these important tasks to begin…

The Young Friends Start Work

The Children of the Sun now had a heavy burden on their shoulders, one for which they would have to do their utmost. They knew that this was something they should have discussed the previous night, and it was for this reason that Ay invited her friends to her house.

Meanwhile, news of the young people's meeting with the elders spread throughout the village. At last, something would happen, and the villagers' bad luck would change for the better. A group of brilliant and extraordinary youngsters would come up with and carry out projects on their behalf. The positive atmosphere, which had come to the village with the return of the group from the mountain, continued. But what were the Children of the Sun planning to do?

As most were without work, this was of particular interest to the village's youth. they wondered whether these new projects could provide new job opportunities for them. The younger children were interested too. Their futures weren't clear. Would they now have a chance to stay in the village when they grew up?

It was evening and nearly dinner time. The youngsters went to Ay's home. She had prepared a place under the arbour, where they congregated at a round table and sipped from glasses of sherbet. As usual, it was Güneş who took the lead: "First of all, we need to agree on a strategy, or else we'll end up drowning in too many problems." Gök agreed: "That's absolutely right. To me, this is the best way. We could follow Grandfather Sun's advice and I think we should start by discussing what he told us in his speech... and take his suggestions on board. We actually saw and learned what we've got to do while we were on the mountain."

Doğa agreed, "So, what we have to do now is to focus on how we can make these things happen here, in the village." "You're right, Doğa," Su continued, "but I think, first of all, we have to find some money for these projects. How can we implement them without any resources?" Now it was Güneş who spoke: "All of what you're saying is true. Alright, to begin with we should look at the village's resources and its potential. But right now, everything we're working with is simply an idea. If they're not supported by local resources, we can't turn our ideas into reality."

Their discussions continued until late. Finally, they agreed on a course of action that they believed would take them in the right direction. Güneş drew together the threads of their debate: "So, if these projects are carried out in the village, the work will have to be done by the locals with us helping them. It's therefore essential that we work together in harmony. Our first principle must, therefore,   be: *with the people, for the people.*"

Everyone liked this idea. It was a principle they all agreed was really important. They took the decision to carry out a survey by holding a series of meetings, through which they could learn the villagers' points of view. "I would like to propose a second principle," said Su. "As far as we know, this village has had its own culture and tradition for more than a thousand years.

"Despite the fact that there is a council and a village Muhtar, the important decisions are made by local people in the village square. We could use this convention for our projects, too. In this way, everyone will have the chance to take part in these projects. Our second principle should be: *the project is carried out in accordance with democratic values.*" This was important too, so Su's proposal was accepted unanimously.

"In that case, I would like to offer a third principle," said Ay.

"There have been in the region of fifteen civilizations in Anatolia and these civilizations have advanced the progress of humankind. However, because of outside influences on our culture, it has begun to disappear. Instead of foreign cultures we should protect and develop our own. Our third principle could, therefore, be: *Anatolian village culture should be explored in depth and this culture should be studied for its widespread use and application.*"

The young comrades agreed to this principle too. It could never be right to replace the rich culture of Anatolia by emulating foreign ones. Each "original project" should only be carried out in accordance with the village's unique culture.

Doğa, who had studied biology and ecology, was very sensitive about protecting nature and the environment. "Anatolian villages are very rich in biodiversity. Our village is in a region near the Caucasus, which is the fifth richest area in the world for flora and fauna. If you look carefully, you'll see that nearly everything that forms part of the village culture has been created using local plants and materials. Yet, these natural beauties and riches have started to disappear; whether by pollution or being destroyed. For this reason, I offer a new principle: *Importance will be given to the preserving of natural beauty and bio-diversity and the maintaining of the culture relating to them.*" Nobody objected to Doğa's suggestion either.

Gök was the last to speak: "I suggest that we put an end to pollution, especially air pollution. For this, I suggest that we should avoid the use of fossil fuels in the village. If we develop new systems for every area that will prevent the production of carbon, this will set a good example for our villagers. Our principle relating to this could be: *In every situation, all efforts will be made to establish social and economic systems based on the sun.*" This principle was also accepted. In this way, the five principles relating to the projects that would be carried out in the village were decided and it was agreed that they would work in accordance with them.

They then discussed the itinerary and drew up a road map. They would carry out a survey to learn the villagers' opinions and expectations. Later, when they were deciding on which projects to undertake, they would take all these into account. Each project would be developed, the project teams selected and the topics they were going to cover would be stated. Finally, they agreed to start their projects only after finding the necessary financial support.

Everybody was happy with the result and returned home to start preparations.

CHAPTER 3

A Quest

Embracing the Village

The next day, the young friends gathered in the square. Using the road map, they'd drafted, they divided the jobs between them and began immediately. Working in two groups, each went their separate way.

This village, formerly known as Vargel, was in the Caucasians and surrounded by mountains and forests. At 1500 meters above sea level, it really was as pretty as a picture postcard.

Located in a valley, the forested areas of the village were mainly of pine and fir trees. The springs that provided fresh water for the village and its neighbours originated in the highland pastures above the valley. Gushing water coursed around the village, forming streams and eventually a river that left the valley, heading north.

The village was situated on the northern side of this valley. All the houses had a southerly or south-easterly aspect and it was possible to see the valley from each house. None of the houses overshadowed its neighbour and each house had a large garden, an orchard and a vegetable patch. The people living in the houses were able to see what was going on in the valley and who was entering or leaving the village. Anyone who needed help could be quickly spotted too. There were so many advantages with this kind of settlement. It also meant that everybody could establish their routine accordingly.

As it happens, this style of settlement was not unique to this village. Similar styles could be seen in other parts of Anatolia. Settlements built on slopes facing the sun are able to make the best use of solar energy. These days, some architects use a similar style for their projects but alas, many of today's urban planners and architects do not and their plans fail to take into account either natural assets or climate. They don't take advantage of the sun, nor do they take care to protect nature and, even if these plans are considered to be important, they are never applied. However, modern city planners should definitely use and protect this important architectural heritage.

Thanks to their education and what they had witnessed and experienced on Sun Mountain, the Children of the Sun were extremely aware of these issues and, for as long as they were working in the village, they would never ignore them. Güneş and Ay wanted to find out more about the life in the past, by visiting the oldest couple in the village.

Mehmet Dede and Ayşe Nine welcomed them with great affection. The young pair hugged these two dears and kissed them before settling on cushions that had been placed in the garden. Ayşe Nine and Mehmet Dede were already well into their nineties but even so, they were in excellent health. First of all, before the conversation got under way, Güneş and Ay thanked the couple for their warm welcome and hospitality and asked them how they were.

It was Ay who raised the first question: "We have many people in this village who are more than ninety years old. It is quite a bit higher than in the general population. We would very much like to learn your secret."

Mehmet Dede answered at once: "I think it's related to the fact that we work. We still get up early and go to bed early.

57

We're never idle: we're always doing something, unlike many in the cities. Physically, our lives are much more active." Ayşe Nine continued: "In my opinion, it's also about our diet; what we eat. We don't eat anything that's grown in towns and cities or produced in factories. We eat and drink natural product that's grown in the village. In this way, the food we eat is really very different." Ay asked the couple: "So, if you don't buy your food and drink, do you produce it all yourselves?"

"In the past," said Mehmet Dede, "everything was grown here in the village and what we didn't grow or produce ourselves we could buy from our neighbours or nearby villages. Now, this is much more difficult. At one time, wheat was grown and threshed in the village; we used to grind our own in the village mill. This is no longer possible, although we do still grow our own fruit and vegetables. We have cows too and still produce our own milk, yogurt, cheese,   and butter. Our chickens, which live free in the garden, provide us with eggs.

"Once upon a time, every family knew how to produce everything themselves. And their knowledge wasn't just limited to producing food either. We used to make our own clothes and build our own houses. Everyone had a different range of skills. These days, there are lots of people who can't even sew on a button." He then drew Ay's attention to a very important issue, that, in modern societies, many people go through life without producing anything themselves. The number of people who can't even produce their own basic needs and who are becoming more and more inactive is gradually increasing. As a result, health problems are becoming ever more widespread.

"In the old days," recalled Mehmet Dede, "nobody in the village was overweight. Not even one person. Although some were getting on in years, they were all trim, strong, quick on their feet and healthy. We rarely saw any illness in our village either but nowadays a great many of the elderly are frail and have a variety of ailments. We're even seeing new diseases; ones that we've never seen before."[2]

Nodding in agreement, Ayşe Nine confirmed what he'd said: "That's so true. I think the secret of our long lives depends a great deal on what we eat and drink. Everything we consume comes from our mountains and forests. As a mountain village, livestock farming was both a source of income and our food. On the pristine mountain pastures, our animals grazed on various kinds of plants and flowers, which we also believe to be health-giving remedies. In this way, the meat and milk of these animals, which contained traces of these natural medicines, protected us from illnesses and helped us to live long and healthy lives. That's why, amongst our ancestors, there were many who lived to well beyond ninety. It's because of this, we were called "Sağlam" and indeed, this [meaning "Strong" in Turkish] is the surname that was given to our family!"

Mehmet Dede picked up on this topic: "Did you know, according to the latest research, there are thousands of different plants on our mountains that can be used to treat many ailments? This proves just how good our diet used to be. But we didn't just benefit from these herbal remedies through the animal products we ate, we used them in our cooking too. Much of the food we – my wife and I – still eat is still made using these plants, herbs,   and fruits that we gather from the mountains and dry or preserve. We also use them to make

---

[2] *Scientific research conducted in the mountain village of Beydili identified seven previously unseen illnesses and concluded that these occurred due to the village's dislocation and modernisation. Source: Beydili cultural village Project; Ç. Göksu, written records taken from the Ministry of Forestry and İsparta governorship.*

conserves, like preserves, pastille, and molasses, which we eat during the winter months."

The things that the elderly couple were saying reminded Güneş of the Legends of the City, which he had heard about before. Why do people live so long in the Caucasus? This was something about which people had been curious for ages, so much so that people visited the region's villages and studies were made of the inhabitants. Finally, it was decided that the reason these villagers lived such long lives was because their diet was so rich in yogurt and milk.

However, now it would appear that this wasn't the whole story. Ayşe Nine, who had come to the village from the Caucasian region, was very aware of all this. Rather than simply milk and yogurt, the secret to their long lives is related to the rich biodiversity of the Caucasian region and their food which they make with the vast range of herbs and plants. Of course, there is another bitter truth; these days, the yogurt we buy from shops has so many additives…

The young friends suddenly had a flash of inspiration. First, they looked at Ayşe Nine, then they looked at each other. Ayşe Nine had just described the wonderful secrets of her long life so eloquently. The youngsters had benefitted much from the wise words of Ayşe Nine and Mehmet Dede and they departed feeling very happy with their newly acquired knowledge.

Although this was their village, there was still so much they weren't aware of. It also began to dawn on them that there was still much more to learn, and this was information they should be sharing. What's more, they realised that the time had come for them to do something about it. [3]

---

[3] As a scientist and published author who has extensively researched village cultures in various regions across Anatolia, including the Caucasus, Taurus and Central Anatolian Mountain Ranges, I would like my readers to know that they will never find any other villages of such cultural wealth and bio-diversity as ours, wherever they travel in the world.

The Sun in the village

Gök and Su were visiting another one of the houses in the village. Knocking on Emine Teyze's door, she opened it and invited them inside. First of all, they passed through an enchanting garden. On entering her home, they saw a short passageway, ending in a staircase. On the left was a living room and a dark kitchen, while on the right was a bedroom and what looked like a small workshop.

Climbing the stairs to the first floor, they came to the *çardak,* which is a large area shaded by vines and surrounded by trellis, with two rooms at the rear and a storeroom. The ground floor was built in stone, while the first floor was made from wood. The space between the inner and outer walls had been packed with soil, for added insulation. Orhon Usta welcomed Su and Gök, inviting them to take a seat on the floor cushions opposite him. They all smiled at each other, and glasses of tea were offered and walnut sweetmeats, which Ayşe Teyze had made herself and placed on a low round table, called a *sofra.*

Now their conversation could begin in earnest. Orhon Usta began by asking: "To what do we owe this agreeable visit?" Before replying, Gök paused for a moment, glancing at his friend: "You are one of the most celebrated master craftsmen of this village and we'd very much appreciate your telling us something about what you do." Teasing the young pair, Emine Teyze quipped: "Why? Do you two want to become builders too then?" Smiling, Su replied, "Actually, no." Then, more seriously, she continued: "That's not why we're here and to be honest, it's not something we've given any thought to. But, as you've mentioned it, why not? It is a great profession!"

Gök spoke up again: "I certainly think we should be repairing our houses in keeping with the original ones. At the moment, we're planning new projects, new buildings. We would like to be able to benefit from your experience. Would that be possible?" "Of course, it would," said Orhon Usta. "We'll do everything we can to help you."

Orhon Usta was one of several very experienced master craftsmen in the area. In addition to him, there was Mehmet Usta, who was a carpenter and also Kader Usta, a stonemason, who worked with Orhon Usta and it would be possible to find others who would help them, too. Most of the houses in the village had been built by these skilled craftsmen and although they were highly talented, they were no longer young. The time had come for them to pass on their skills to the young villagers.

Su then asked Orhon Usta a question, which she initiated by describing the village as she saw it. "When I look at the houses, I can't help noticing that they all look over the valley, and that every house faces south, benefiting from direct sunlight. You can see them from the valley. All of them are positioned on the hillside, like gems. They're all so beautiful. They use nature to the best effect, and all of them are aesthetically pleasing. What do *you* think is the secret of their beauty and harmony?"

Orhon Usta was delighted that the young friends were passionate about the village architecture, not least because others who had left their villages didn't appear to like the traditional houses and buildings. When these people returned to their villages, they said that they preferred the urban style, and wanted to have concrete homes instead. Orhon Usta disliked this kind of construction and criticised those who built them. But even so, when these people came back their villages, they built themselves reinforced concrete houses. So

63

far, there were four or five houses like this, which infuriated the craftsmen. Therefore, it was good to finally hear that there were young people who appreciated the time-honored village architecture.

"We're delighted you like traditional houses," said Orhon Usta. "So, I'd like to take this opportunity to explain the secrets of my profession. First of all, to build something like this requires skills that are passed from father to son over many centuries. It's therefore essential that these skills are passed on to our young generation. In a nutshell, the culture of this architecture involves a wealth of knowledge that has been developed over time, and we are trying to remain as loyal as we can to these principles."

Orhon Usta looked at the youngsters steadily. He spoke with gravity: "This knowledge is both general and specific. The main rules are always to use natural materials, make the most of the sun and to locate the houses on the hillside, overlooking the valley. People who don't follow these rules can't be thought of as master craftsmen."

He carefully explained how, in the old days, people never built houses that didn't have a garden or face the sun. But over time, new architects and builders had come along. Now, not only were they especially keen to use concrete, their buildings did not reflect Anatolian culture in the slightest, and they were leaving a destructive trail of once fine traditional buildings in their wake. The young people had grown up in these village houses and had also lived in concrete buildings in the city. They knew the difference very well.

The elderly craftsman explained how, in Le Corbusier's book, Urbanism, the famous architect had praised Istanbul's traditional architecture, while describing New York as a bad example of a city and one that shouldn't be used as a model.

64

Many talented western craftsmen and architects, the Usta said, have admired Anatolia's unique architecture, which varies from region to region according to the climate and culture. However, admiration for Western architecture in Anatolia has resulted in it being gratuitously copied in the country's villages, towns and cities.

Traditional principals, once considered so essential and which depend on the sun and harmony with nature, are no longer being taken into consideration and as a result energy consuming cities, lacking originality and aesthetics, are being built. The young friends were already aware of this situation and there was much they wanted to learn from the master craftsmen. Gök intervened: "We've noticed that wood is often preferred as a fuel for stoves in traditional houses, while coal or oil is generally used in modern concrete ones. What do you think is the reason for this?"

The craftsman knew the answer: "These days, people aren't building energy-saving houses. They can't. So, the natural ways of heating and cooling homes, once used in Anatolian architecture, are no longer being applied. When you compare the modern concrete homes built in recent years with traditional ones, you'll notice that they're consuming eight or ten times more energy. Building this kind of traditional architecture relies on knowledge and experience."

"What would you say is the most noticeable difference between traditional houses and modern ones, then?" Gök asked.

"Surely you can see how hideous most of these new buildings are?" Orhon Usta replied, somewhat tetchily. "Buildings used to have aesthetic principles and harmony but nowadays each is different and ugly. Buildings used to complement each other but new buildings look like blots on the landscape. Don't you agree?"

Orhon Usta mentioned many other differences between old and new buildings too, but he left the most important one until last: "Village houses were not only homes, they were productive workshops. Many of the things a family needed used to be made at home. In these houses, there were various suitable areas for preparing and storing food for winter.

For example, there was the *çardak* where we dried our fruits and vegetables and stored them for the winter. Also, there was a place to prepare and cook food inside the house, and another one in the garden. Each house had a barn too where all the winter provisions could be stored. You won't find any of these in new houses."

An interesting thought occurred to Su: *In the old days, people were called producers; now they're called consumers: two perspectives that couldn't be more different!* The youngsters had been listening intently to the elderly man and his inspiring words left them silent, thoughtful; so, the Usta continued: "Nowadays, few people realise that every house has invisible social and psychological differences. Of these, the foremost is the philosophical outlook of the Anatolian people, their concept of life." To be honest, they had not expected such interesting explanations from Orhon Usta and now he was moving onto the philosophical approach. They were mesmerised and couldn't take their eyes off him.

"As you may have noticed," the wise old man continued, "each house has a guest room. It is customary for these rooms to be rather well decorated; we say they're dressed 'like a bride,' with traditional kilims, colourful rugs, cushions and so on. They're usually the best rooms in the house, even if they aren't used very often and they're reserved for guests. Guests, whether they are known well or not, are always considered to be blessed. People are delighted to welcome guests into their homes and always happy to prepare the best food

66

they can for them and be the ultimate host. I don't think there's anywhere else in the world that has a similar custom. This is such a valued tradition amongst Turks and a world-view of humanity that Anatolian people have continued from the past to the present; in a way, it's about putting their philosophy of humankind into practice."

While he was telling the youngsters about the architecture of his village, this "master of masters" was also describing the exceptional philosophy of the villagers; one that had reached to a level way beyond that of contemporary society.

In fact, they were now beginning to understand just how different these villagers were from people who consider themselves to be modern. After all, don't people these days tend to be more interested in money and possessions? Don't they actually worship materialism as some kind of wealth in itself? Aren't they competitive, unethical? Do they really ever put others before themselves? Where is humanity in today's world? Where are those who live in harmony with the natural world? Where are those who respect nature, those who value others, who actually take pleasure in living side by side with other people? Where are they? But aren't all of these things intrinsically part of the very essence of the Anatolian people? Aren't the people of our village just like that? And isn't this organic, humanistic philosophy not reflected in our architecture?

Su wanted to ask one more question: "We have seen the secret garden of the sun," she said, almost whispering. "We've visited the holy city of the sun with the Wise Ones of the Sun. We've stayed in the most advanced solar houses."[4]. Returning to her normal voice, she asked Orhon Usta, "So, how and

---

[4] *These are discussed in my novel, The Mysterious Garden of the Sun*

67

where do you make the most of the sun in village houses?" "Well", the sage replied with characteristic modesty, "Next to what you've just seen, the things we do are undoubtedly very modest and unassuming. We've just heard what you've told us, but we haven't had a chance to see this for ourselves. Even so, we'll do our best with what we've figured out. I can tell you what that is, if you want."

The youngsters did want to hear his thoughts, as they needed to know to what extent the villagers could benefit from the sun. Orhon Usta took a deep breath, as if to begin, but Emine Teyze pre-empted him: "It's the sun! The sun!" she cried. "The village needs the sun, and the sun sustains the village. The sun means everything for the village. We go to bed with the sun and rise with the sun. At night, when there's no sun, everything falls silent. The streets are dark and wild creatures prowl around the village. No one goes outside unless they have to. But when the sun rises, everything changes."

Pausing momentarily to take a breath, the elderly woman continued with as much passion as before. "The village is liberated from the pitch darkness of the night and shakes off the morning chill. With the sun, daily life can resume. You could say, every day we die and every day we're reborn with the sun. When the sun rises, we, along with all the plants and animals, are re-energized. The sounds of animals and human voices resonate in the air. Herdsmen head to the hills, while other folk set off for their gardens and fields. Back in the village, women light fires; get breakfast and prepare food. To put it simply, the village falls asleep with the sun, it dies; gets up with the sun, it's resurrected."

No one, apart from Emine Teyze that is, would have been able to describe the significance of the sun in village life in a way that was so short and sweet, yet compelling: "Our village is way up high. The sun that shines during the summer months means more to us than the sea and the plains. During the long winter days, we still make use of those sunny summer months. We grow fruit and vegetables that are ideal for our alpine climate. And, thanks to the sun, we're able to harvest and dry these before storing them in our barns and cellars. Our animals graze on our mountains and highland pastures. So, our winter food comes from these herb-rich, grassy meadows. The animals we eat, everything we eat and drink during the winter, is provided by the sun. By the way, our sun preserves, and molasses are truly legendary."

What Emine Teyze was saying reminded the youngsters of their days in the city. They thought about all the people who still don't appreciate what the sun is and are unable to imagine its value. Also, having moved far away from the countryside, these people are no longer aware of the value of plants and nature either. These people's minds are distracted by materialism and abstract beliefs, distant from the core values of life. They've forgotten they are natural beings and have taken refuge in bogus identities and values. They've forgotten the vast wealth of the sun and nature. According to them, Emine Teyze was nothing more than an ignorant and illiterate peasant woman; whereas, her world view and philosophy of life was in fact much more realistic, and up there with those of the scientists.

Slowly, Gök turned to Orhon Usta: "Well, the beautiful way that Emine Teyze has explained the importance of the sun in the village has left us totally stunned. Perhaps you could now tell us how house architecture benefits from the sun?" A smile slowly spread across Orhon Usta's face, as he spent a few moments thinking what he was going to say; clearly, he was trying to organize his thoughts.

Finally, the Usta composed himself and looking at the young friends, he said: "You're right. I'm also truly amazed by what

Emine Teyze has said. And, even as she was speaking, I had already begun to think about the houses we build. I was recalling how we make them, and I can tell you this: just like our village lifestyle, our domestic architecture is also totally dependent on the sun. Look, we build houses and their gardens on northern hillsides, on high ground, so they're facing south. In this way they get more sun. Both the houses and the gardens can benefit from direct sunlight. The garden terrace gets the sun. Even in winter, thanks to the sun, we are able to use every area for different purposes. The garden is in direct sunlight and by growing them under cover, we can plant our seedlings earlier."

Orhon Usta continued: "The situation in the home is no different. Inside and outside living areas, as well as workspaces, get sunlight. Each house has a sunroom; built so as to get direct sunlight. Even in winter, on sunny days this room becomes warm, so there is no need to use any other fuel. Family members are therefore able to live in this room without having to light the stove. What's more, they can sleep in this room at night. Using this room saves energy. And there's the çardaks, of course, which are positioned in such a way that they too can be heated by the sun."

"That's great! So, what kinds of fuel are being used in these homes, apart from the sun?"

Orhon Usta hesitated, saying a quiet: "I think there is something..." before continuing. "Last year, I visited one of my friends at his new concrete house in the village. He was constantly burning coal to heat his home, but even so, the house still felt cold. I could feel waves of cold energy coming from the north-facing walls. When I touched one, it was so cold, I was really shocked. The wall was cooling the house like an air conditioner. The north-facing walls of a concrete building are cold to the touch. They become frozen, making the room

70

feel even colder. Now, if north facing walls were buried in the ground, they wouldn't be cold to the touch and the house wouldn't become cold, either. Quite the reverse in fact, the rooms would stay warm. Interestingly enough, such homes could actually benefit from the warmth of the soil."

The Usta looked happy as he shared this positive information about the village's architectural culture. The youngsters glanced at each other, before Gök spoke again: "Now we'd like to share another piece of fascinating information, something we learned from the Wise Ones of the Sun. As far as we're aware, you're burning wood for additional heat. In this wood there is the solar energy that trees capture from the thousands of leaves that absorb it over the years. In other words, there is solar energy in this wood; people who burn wood, are heating their houses with the energy of the sun."

Gök continued: "There's also another heating system I've come across in your house. Your kitchen is like a large room. It's surrounded by thick walls and has a small window. The north facing wall is buried in the earth. When the stove is lit, to cook food or boil water, it heats the kitchen too. What's more, you have placed the cooker against the north facing wall and located the chimney inside the wall. When the stove is ablaze, the wall is heated not only by the ground but also by the burning wood. This wall is like a "thermal wall" that warms the whole house."

Emine Teyze and Orhon Usta were delighted by this visit and Gök and Su also felt happy. The village would finally begin to learn the secrets of their wonderfully natural and beautiful homes. The young friends departed, feeling tremendously elated.

Opportunities

Doğa and Can wanted to visit a newly married couple to hear their opinions. Can, who had studied archaeology, had returned to his village but was now unemployed. He was Doğa's childhood friend. They liked each other and used to meet and chat from time to time. The gate was opened by the newlyweds, Aysun and Mert, who led their visitors to the garden, where they all sat on divans. Aysun, who came from a different neighbourhood, had come to the village as a bride, so she was getting to grips with living in her new home.

She'd previously attended a sewing course and had also learned how to weave kilims and carpets, for which she'd earned a certificate. In addition to this, they were renovating the house, which Mert had inherited from his father. Nearly every part of the house was being renewed. They had also added a new kilim and carpet workshop to the west facing part of the house. After drinking their tea, Doğa and Can asked to see the workshop. Aysun accompanied them, while explaining what they wanted to do.

"We've got a workshop. But we haven't started working in it yet. Our plan is to educate and teach the girls sewing and kilim and carpet weaving, so we can work together. The young people I've already spoken with are really enthusiastic. We'll begin once the workshop is completed."

Mert said that they had a few acres of land, where they grew fruit and vegetables. His plan for the future was to contribute towards the establishment of an agricultural business in the village.

As they all sat around the table, an intense discussion began. While many of the village's youngsters were moving to the city, Mert and his family had chosen to remain in the village.

Can and Doğa, were relieved to hear this. Doğa, asked the first question: "If everyone else is moving to the city, why did you decide to come back to the village? Why do you want to be here?" Mert was not slow in replying: "I was born and grew up in this village. I learned about farming and agriculture from my parents. Yes... I have been to the city, I studied there. But I never liked city life, never liked being there. City life doesn't appeal to us."

"Why is that?" asked Can. "It's because I'm a person who loves living free," answered Mert, spreading his arms wide, as he did so, in a kind of embrace. "That's something I could never be if I was working in the city for somebody else. Here I'm my own boss. I'm working and producing for myself. Here I'm not a slave, I can make my own plans. What more can I say? ...There's nobody forcing me to work."

"I agree with Mert," confirmed Aysun. "Here I can establish my own workshop and do my own business. Also, the air in the village is much cleaner and the people are friendly and sincere. This kind of life suits us." Cheerful grins spread across everyone's faces. Still smiling, they all rose and went upstairs to the çardak, where Aysun showed Doğa and Can what she'd already achieved. She laid out the carpets and kilims she'd made. It would not be an exaggeration to say that each one was a work of art. The kilims were woven using motifs from the region and the colours she'd used were vibrant. All this could mean only one thing; when the machines and looms were finally installed, it would become an exceptional workshop.

As Doğa and Can left the house, they felt happy about the new possibilities they had seen and heard. There were things that should definitely be discussed. While walking along the road, they bumped into Hasan Dede, one of the villages elders. He invited the youngsters to his home. For many years,

73

Hasan Dede had had his own carpentry workshop. But it had been closed long ago. Can and Doğa now opened the door of his workshop, walked in and carefully examined what they saw.

Inside there was every kind of woodwork tool. At the centre of the workshop there was a long bench on which was a mechanical saw. Hanging neatly on the walls, were saws, chisels, a complete set of screwdrivers and drilling tools. Doğa asked the obvious, as if it were a question: "So, you've closed your workshop?" Dede responded in a low, measured tone: "I have two children. I raised them both to be carpenters. As most people have left the village, there was no one to give them any work. They became unemployed and had to move to the city. They wanted to take me too, but I couldn't face leaving here. What can I do in the city at my age? How could I get used to it? Since my wife died, I've been trying to survive alone."

There was a deep sadness in his voice and a sense of abandonment. The youngsters felt his melancholy and tried to comfort him. "Please, don't be sad. You'll soon see our village return to life and plenty of new opportunities will arise for you and the other villagers." On the way back, it was Doğa who finally spoke: "As far as I can see, people are generally feeling hopeless and miserable. Apart from a few people, nobody knows what to do. In spite of this, there are loads of opportunities in the village to make things. There are old workshops and the elderly craftspeople. I hope we'll be able to bring all this together."

Divided into groups, over the next three days the young companions visited the houses individually and had long conversations with the villagers. When this had been completed, they got together again. Joined by Can and Ayben, the young friends assessed the situation.

74

The Atmosphere in the Village

The companions were gathered at Su's house to review the village's current situation. It was no longer the community it had once been. The population had declined; for the most part, only the elderly remained, and production had ground to a halt. There was none of the old vitality. The village was down in the dumps, enveloped in misery; it was becoming as dead as a graveyard... Morale had collapsed, hopes were shattered.

The depressing events of recent years were not limited to migration alone. The negative aspects of modern civilization were also impacting on the village. The use of artificial fertilisers, toxic chemicals, coal, and petrol was increasing, slowly but surely polluting both the soil, the air and the water. Each new concrete building was effectively a monument to this dreadfulness. If measures weren't taken soon, nothing would remain of the old way of life.

To assess the situation, the youngsters needed to carry out a case study, as, in order to protect and revitalise the village culture it would be necessary to develop a plan for a "new village." This would have to be one that retained useful cultural aspects from the past, while at the same time contributing to the development of a village that was more progressive, prosperous and advanced.

The group's task would be really difficult. It would not be enough to save this one village or carry out a limited project. They would have to develop a new village that could be used as an example; one that would provide inspiration for all the other villages in Anatolia. The young companions had a good grasp of what needed to be done. They decided to create a suitable model that would maintain and develop the legacy of human values in a way that protected their core ideologies.

In short, they decided to create a universal village, and build it right here, in their community.

It was Atatürk who personally established a model for exploring and advancing Anatolian village culture and he was the first person to do so. But unfortunately, by the 1950s, unplanned and unregulated urban migration had led to major ordeals for the country. Anatolia's villages were dying, and unplanned urban sprawl had begun to appear. At the same time, the rich culture of Anatolia's towns and villages started to disappear.

Authentic villages, which were thought to still exist by the thousand, would have to be protected. Blighted villages had to be taken in hand with a new approach, and their economies revived. The young group would have to do this hard work, work that should be done by the state, by themselves. Together with the villagers...

Güneş made a suggestion: "We've identified the village's main problems and learned about some of the possibilities. Now it's time to construct its future. Together with the villagers, we must create and focus on a residential prototype that protects its nature and its culture. It should also be one that includes features that could be used as examples for other villages. "You're right" said Gök. "The values we've identified here go way beyond being merely local ones. These are related to village culture and biodiversity in the Caucasian region of Anatolia. For this reason, we can and should be able to get support from universities and other countries, which will in turn take our projects to a national and international level."

"We could begin by putting an end to environmental pollution," said Doğa. "In order to stop it, I think we need to protect our village from external influences. Our mission should be to stop harmful activities and prevent dangerous substances coming into our village; for example, we should prohibit chemicals and artificial fertilizers that are damaging for our health." There were a great many questions for which the youngsters would have to find answers and provide solutions. On what basis could new systems be established, to change the underlying social economic structures that were causing the village to decline?

Architecturally speaking, the traditional village buildings were extremely precious. Yet most were close to collapse, as they hadn't been used for ages. Some of the houses had already been demolished as they were uninhabitable and those that survived were seriously neglected. How could they protect the traditional village architecture? How could the resources be found for their restoration? The village squares and communal areas had not been taken care of for a long while either, so they were also in dire need of repair.

The economic structure of the village was in a bad way. It was impossible for the villagers to contribute to these requirements out of their own pockets; they could scarcely provide for themselves. Vegetable and fruit growing, as well as animal husbandry, were on the way out. To put it bluntly, it was going to be very hard to regenerate the village economy. For the Children of the Sun there would be difficult times ahead.

The village's social life was slowly dying: several associations had already been closed, and cooperatives had been disbanded. There was certainly no traditional nightlife left in the village. Everyone had already given up on the culture of going out for the evening or visiting their neighbours. Nowadays, everybody stayed in and many were obsessed with watching television. Making handicrafts was almost a thing of the past. Needlework, carpet and kilim weaving, carpentry and so on, all crafts that had once been done at home, were for the most part no more. How could they revive these skills and pastimes? How could they be used to provide an income?

The ancient transhumance – Yörük - custom of making the annual trek to the highland pastures for the summer months, which had once played such an important role in village life, had all but ended. As they no longer made this journey with their animals to the highlands and mountains, these grass-lands were left unused.

Taking all these issues into consideration, the youngsters worked until first light. Then, discussing each project one by one, they added them to the village roadmap. Now, even though it was still at the discussion stage, the village finally had a plan. It was time to act.

Preparations

The youngsters needed to speak with the village Muhtar and the council and share their ideas for the project with them. It was almost evening by the time they met up at the Muhtar's house. Güneş put the map on the wall and was first to speak; using the map to describe the various projects. He provided detailed information about the regeneration of village life, the organisation of social and creative activities, the proper restoration of the traditional houses, the construction of roads and the production of fruit and vegetables; explaining how each project related to them, individually.

One of the elders said: "This is great! You've touched on nearly everything. But the real problem still remains... the village is seriously strapped for cash. So, how do we find the resources to carry all this out? How do we find the money? "You're right, of course," admitted Gök. "First we have to get funding. For this, I believe we have two options. One is to find a lump sum, enough to cover all the projects; the other one is to find separate resources for each one. It's probably too difficult to find a lump sum; it would be easier to find small amounts, separate funding, for each project. What's more, in addition to getting adequate funding, we also need a management team to work on these projects. This is an issue that the council should decide but both project management and funding must be done legally."

At this point, there was a short break, during which the elders spoke with each other about the issues the youngsters had suggested. This proved to be rather lengthy but, in the end, they reached a unanimous decision, and a vote was passed to establish a Village Project Management Committee and Village Development Fund. A decision was made: the youngsters and Güneş would head the team and carry out the management of the village project. With regard to the Village Development fund, they decided that each project would be allocated ten percent of the funding. Also, all grants and resources relating to the project would be placed in the fund and the money would be used in this way.

The young companions were delighted. By giving them total authority over the projects, the village council obviously trusted them. They knew that they had taken on a huge responsibility. Would they be able to handle such a burden? Yet, the young friends trusted in the villagers. Wasn't it villagers like these who had managed and maintained the village for hundreds of years?

The day's decisions were immediately announced over the village's tannoy system. With these projects, a new era was dawning for the village community, and they were ones that would be carried out by the villagers' new heroes. Everybody believed in them. But even so, some doubts remained. How would the youngsters find the necessary resources when various people and even the state hadn't been able to do so? Many times, the villagers had applied to the state for assistance but with no success. Also, people who had left the village did not bother to invest in it; usually preferring to devote their money to the places where they now lived. The authorities had left these villages to their fate. How could such projects be put into practice without state support? But even so, a faint light could still be seen on the horizon.

It was not long before details of the meeting, and the decisions made, had spread throughout the village. The following night the villagers began to gather in Fire Square. Hearing this, the young friends joined them. The eternal flame was revived and then everybody began congratulating the youngsters and asking them a great many questions. No longer just the project of the Children of the Sun, it had become the village's too. Everybody made themselves comfortable and the discussion began.

The village Muhtar was the first to speak. Indicating Güneş and his companions, the Muhtar proclaimed: "Our village now has a project team and here are the young people who'll be working on it. In spite of the difficult circumstances they face, I trust they'll be successful. We all have complete faith in our young comrades."

Following this introduction, the Muhtar explained each project in turn. As he concluded, the villagers gave him a standing ovation. The applause was a clear sign of how important all this was for these people, who had long been living in hardship. It felt as if there was finally a glimmer of hope in the darkness. Although Güneş and his friends were slightly overwhelmed by the approval everyone was showing, it boosted their confidence and made them feel much stronger.

Meanwhile, the villagers were wondering why the youngsters were taking on such a difficult task. Although the mothers and fathers were counting on their children studying hard and getting a good education, sending them off to the city to achieve this, they also quietly hoped they would return to their villages to work, marry and have children of their own. But alas, so far none had chosen to return. The young companions were the first to decide to stay and choose to do something for their village. It was clear from the villagers' faces just how happy and excited they were. It was for all these reasons, that the applause lasted so long. As everyone settled back into their seats, a hush descended.

Now it was time for the Children of the Sun to speak. Deeply impressed by the villagers' attentiveness, Güneş rose to his feet. There was a great deal that needed to be said… but what should it be and how should it be conveyed? They were only at the beginning, so he shouldn't give them too much hope. In the past, politicians and leaders of the various political parties had visited them and made promises to develop the village, but these had soon been forgotten. He and his young friends did not want to end up in the same situation. At least in this case, the work they were planning to do was not only their ideas but those of the villagers too. These projects were ones in which everyone's participation and support was essential; otherwise, they would be impossible to carry out.

Finally, Güneş began to speak. In a measured tone, he said: "These projects are, in truth, not just our suggestions; they're also very closely linked to your own expectations. As you know, we have been speaking with you over many days. We've asked you what you've already done and what you'd like to see happen. All we've done is to transform your opinions and expectations into projects. We then handed these over to the village Muhtar. For this reason, they are not our projects, they're yours."

What was Güneş saying? Could he mean that these were the villagers' own projects? How could these young people be so modest, so self-effacing? Until now, no one had attached any importance to the villagers' ideas and hopes. They had always been ignored. Everybody usually considered villagers like them to be ignorant. It was the first time that they'd been with people who valued their opinions and took them seriously. They were actually feeling rather proud of themselves and began to listen to the speeches more carefully.

Gök was next to speak: "Our village is one of the most remarkable anywhere in the world. Here in the Caucasian Mountains, people in our village live longer due to their own unique culture and traditions, plants and animals. But sadly, these riches are not appreciated and have been left to their fate. Our goal is to protect this beautiful village inherited from our ancestors and help it prosper. This is why it's so important that your proposals are included in these projects."

Then it was Su's turn: "The village is in a state of ruin; infrastructure is lacking, the roads are neglected. We know that these infrastructural, as well as other related issues, are under state control, so the village management team will apply to the relevant authorities for what's needed. I hope the necessary help will be sent as soon as possible." Doğa continued along the same theme: "The village houses and buildings are among our village's most important cultural treasures. Dilapidated buildings beyond repair need to be cleared and the usable ones need to be repaired at once. There are many young people in our village who can train to do this kind of work. We also know that our village has many skilled craftsmen and builders and we need all of their help for us to be able to achieve this by ourselves."

It was Ay who summed up on behalf of the group: "As long as we work together with passion and enthusiasm, we can achieve our goals and return our village to its former vitality. Now everyone must think about and choose which project they would like to do themselves, or be part of, and let us know. Let's decide together what we can do to make this all happen."

As Ay finished her speech, there was a colossal round of applause. Now everybody was happy.

This meeting was a sign that a new chapter had begun in the village's story. It seemed as if the villages' downfall and setbacks had finally come to an end and beautiful days, filled with love, hope and joy, were about to begin.

Chapter 4

The Sun Culture

The First Step

Three days had passed. Once more the villagers gathered in the square but this time, they were waiting for the ribbon cutting ceremony and the first work to begin. Together, the Muhtar and Ay cut the ribbon: "*Hayırlı olsun!*" they said in unison. "Good luck for our village!" On hearing this, the villagers cheered and clapped. Then everyone proceeded to the garden of a nearby house. Following the ceremony, the crowd dispersed, and the work continued.

The craftsmen and builders' work could now get underway. With the laying of the first foundation stone the first project had finally begun. For Güneş and his friends there had been so much to discuss, but they had ultimately decided to make the first project a traditional village house.

There were many reasons why such as house was necessary. First of all, a place was needed where the projects could be put into practice. They therefore chose to start with the renovation of an uninhabited house near the village square. The building would also provide a place to stay for visitors coming to see the project. Some social activities could be held there as well. However, before the work could begin it was necessary to buy this house. The owners had long left the village and were not planning to return. The current owners were tracked down and the issue explained to them, upon which they happily donated the house to the villagers without a moment's hesitation.

The village's craftsmen got together to decide on the necessary repairs, what materials were needed, and which supplies should be obtained with the money donated by the villagers. Organising a repair team was now essential. They discussed this with Orhon Usta, who explained: "We have a tradition, whereby the village's common property is made communally. That's what we can do here too, so don't worry about it."

Although the youngsters didn't say anything, they were rather apprehensive about this idea of communal labour. But in actual fact, *imece* as it is known, is one of the most important aspects of the co-operative village tradition. All work for the common good used to be done like this, especially when it came to helping orphans or the elderly. An effective form of cooperation, it was once a common social tradition in Anatolia, and one that was used until relatively recently. Unfortunately, this is no longer the case.

Since Western culture began to dominate the country, with values based on individualism and personal interests, these influences also became prevalent in Anatolian villages and, as a result, the culture of cooperation and social understanding had practically disappeared. This was why the Children of the Sun were somewhat apprehensive. While they were eagerly waiting in the Muhtar's house, a request for volunteers was made over the loudspeaker system.

Oh dear! Their worst fears were realised... Apart from the work team only a few volunteers showed up. To begin with there was a sense of hopelessness, but Güneş and his young companions wouldn't give up that easily. A ten-strong team was formed: three builders, two volunteers and themselves. The work would be carried out with two shifts of five. Things finally got underway, on time and with great ceremony.

On the first day, the interior of the house and the garden were cleared. On the second day, thanks to the second team, the

85

crumbling walls were demolished and rebuilt, and the rotting wood was replaced. From time to time, the villagers came to watch, talking quietly amongst themselves. The determination of the young heroes, who were putting their hearts and souls into their work, was having an effect. During the days that followed, one by one, others began to join them and gradually the size of the work teams increased.

Within a few days, the teams had significantly increased in number. With everyone wanting to work, it was as if the village had returned to the old days. Güneş, who was leading the renovation team, evaluated the requests from the volunteers who came forward and organised work schedules. As a result, repairs were progressing fairly rapidly.

A tradition that the village had almost forgotten had begun to return and the sense of solidarity that took hold further strengthened it. This was a hopeful sign. The preservation of the village's cultural heritage was closely associated with the philosophy and worldview that constituted this heritage. They could not revive the social traditions of the village without also revitalising the culture of village life.

In reality, from time to time the state had felt it necessary to step in to protect traditional life and historic buildings in different parts of the country. In connection with this, a conservation law was passed, the legislation for which developed over time. The aim of this law was to protect historic sites and artefacts, natural assets and conservation areas. In spite of this, as this law didn't include old structures and traditional settlements, the most interesting historic cities in our country have continued to disappear together with their traditional configurations.

Apart from limited conservation areas, which form the true identities of Anatolia's city centres, towns have continued to be destroyed due to urban planning practices. Now there is no town or city in Turkey that embodies the country's historical heritage. It's fair to say that Ankara, Istanbul and Izmir in particular, each of which has thousands of years of history, have lost their true identities as a result of mismanagement. It could be argued that they are the main places in which self-seekers and profiteers have become dominant.

Moreover, universities kept quiet as the pillaging, plundering and swamping by concrete persisted. This blight, this degeneracy, has now unfortunately spread to Anatolia's smaller towns and villages... it has become ubiquitous. Could this countrywide cultural carnage be stopped by a new village project that offered the right solutions? Could an excellent example of authenticity, to a large extent, be protected?

The First Project

Although the villagers didn't realise, they had begun building the first solar house; one that was unique to this Turkish village. They would only become aware of this after the building had been completed. Güneş and his friends decided to keep this a secret and only reveal it during the opening ceremony.

Renovations continued at ground level. There used to be a byre under the house and for this reason, it had an earth floor. This would be to their advantage, as the ground floor needed to be built again from scratch, taking thermal conditions into account. But the villagers didn't know this either.

The Children of the Sun's restoration plan was based on insulating the structure – both from heat and cold – using a form of solar energy. There were many reasons for this. The village was 1500 meters above sea level. The winters in this part of the world were long and hard and the village was sometimes snowed-in for months. Heating houses at this altitude was not easy and involved a great deal of energy; however, using the sun could reduce energy consumption by as much as 40%.

Güneş explained: "According to Emine Teyze and Orhon Usta, traditional houses in this village used to be built to make use of the sun. The position of the building, as well as sunny indoor and outdoor spaces, enabled the occupants to live in unison with the sun. This culture came about with experience gained over thousands of years. It is therefore essential that this rich legacy of solar architecture is protected and passed on to the next generation as part of our cultural heritage. This must be our mission."

Su agreed with him: "Yes, it's absolutely vital we protect the sun culture's traditional architecture. But… there was a solar house that we saw and admired on Sun Mountain, although it was much more advanced than these village houses. If we use this for inspiration, I think we'll be able to add new features.

Güneş felt he needed to explain this idea in more detail: "We've done a lot of research on the traditional solar architecture of Anatolia. In Southwestern Anatolia there were advanced sun cities, such as Priene and Solea, where solar houses were built according to the different climate conditions. The levels of achievement differed in each region. For example, although there was 100% success in Cappadocia, the button houses in the Taurus Mountains were 80% successful and it the Erzurum houses about 40%. In short, it is possible to benefit from the rich Sun culture and modern technological innovations throughout Anatolia..."

Inspired by this, Doğa interrupted him in mid-sentence. "So, this means we can minimize energy consumption and reduce the consumption of coal and fuel." But Güneş was ready for him: "No!" he said firmly. "Definitely not. Our aim isn't to *reduce* the use of fuel and coal that pollute the atmosphere and the village; rather, our aim is to do away with polluting sources of energy *altogether*. This is what was done on Sun Mountain and we'll try to do the same with the house we're renovating here." These words delighted everybody. It meant that they would be building the first solar house in Turkey. Gök voiced what everybody was thinking: "In that case, we'll be building the most advanced house in the country."

Once again Güneş responded to this statement with his usual modesty: "Well," he said, "We can but try. If we succeed with this project perhaps it can be used in many other villages too, so it'll be the whole of Anatolia that benefits. But first we have to make this building a success."

The young friends continued with their discussions until morning. As the sun was about rise, Doğa said: "If you like, we won't mention the solar house project. For the time being it can be our secret and we'll tell everyone about it at the opening ceremony." They nodded their heads in agreement. Everyone felt tired but were also very excited: they felt as if the sun's energy had entered their souls.

The First Solar House

The restoration continued rapidly, and the villagers paid frequent visits, watching the developments closely like hawks and often helping out themselves. The Muhtar and the elders also visited, even more regularly. They all thought the youngsters were doing a great job for the village. The biggest changes were on the ground floor. The entrance to the building was going to be here. This floor would also have a large living area and washing and lavatory facilities.

The rear wall of this area would be totally buried but the side walls only partially so. They had to thoroughly clean this area, as it had previously been used as a byer. When this had been done, they dug a pit of about twelve square metres in the middle of the earth floor. This would be the underground depot for storing the solar energy but for now they couldn't tell anyone about it. They also made another change. The covered the buried rear wall with wood, leaving a gap of about ten centimetres.

The Muhtar, who had been watching them carefully, asked Güneş: "What are you doing exactly?" Güneş explained briefly but without giving any specific details of the solar house system. "Our aim is to make this village house into a community centre, something that the villagers think is sorely lacking. It can be a place for them and visitors to meet and somewhere for guests to stay. On the ground floor there will be an information desk, a dining room, a kitchen area and toilet facilities. Visitors will be able to chat, rest and if necessary, they can also have their meals there or entertain themselves.

In fact, they'd needed a place like this for a long time. Visitors from outside the village, especially, had a problem with finding somewhere to stay. "Now, our visitors will have a place to go to," said Güneş. "Everybody who comes to this village will be able to eat, drink and rest there and, if necessary, they'll be able to stay in one of the rooms upstairs. The Muhtar felt happy when he heard this. The house would provide new opportunities that would certainly enrich village life.

The main fabric of the building would not be touched. On the wooden top floor, they packed soil, mixed with straw and organic matter, between the timbers. The four rooms and the çardak were not changed; however, the front of the çardak was enclosed with glazing. The fireplace on the back wall was removed and a new stove, which was also a heating system, was fitted in the middle of the building. Hence, the rooms on both downstairs and upstairs were connected by a chimney. The flues for the solar energy and the additional heating systems were integrated into the same chimney.

Another change was made on the roof. The damaged and collapsed gables were replaced, and retiled. Black tiles were placed on the southern slope of the roof and covered with glass. The roof was insulated, and two additional wooden rooms were added in this space. Also, an exit was made leading to the roof along with two solar panels and two collectors. In this way, traditional solar architecture was supported by new systems.

According to the calculations made, the heating for the building would mostly be provided by solar and thermal energy, while the remaining parts would be heated using wood. If this proved successful it would become a model for houses free from fossil fuels. Nevertheless, they would have to be careful: there were doubts about it staying within the financial estimates.

There were hot air ducts in the building, but none were visible. The link between the solar systems on the roof and the solar storage systems underground were virtually invisible too and no one was really aware of these air flows.

In addition to the house renovations they also had to deal with the garden layout. The gate at the entrance to the garden was repaired. Seating areas were created, and appropriate places were planted with flowers, while solar lamps were put at the entrance and in various parts of the garden.

The restoration was now complete. Indeed, a beautiful and shining example of village architecture had emerged from the ruins. Those who looked at the building appreciated the teams' efforts and didn't hide their admiration. And the villagers were proud of working together and their accomplishment.

Now everyone was waiting for the opening ceremony.

The Opening Ceremony

The Muhtar decided on the opening date and invited the entire village to come along. He also sent invitations to the provincial governor, the town governor and the Muhtars from neighbouring villages. The opening came three days after the completion of the building. Everyone who'd been personally invited, and others who had heard about the opening ceremony flocked to the square, until it was packed to overflowing: no one had expected so many people to attend.

It was the largest crowd the village had ever seen. Only with this were the villagers beginning to realise how far the young friends' accomplishments were spreading, purely by word of mouth. From the size of the crowd it was very apparent that their village was starting to attract a great deal of attention. This made the villagers even more elated; they were working together to create something truly wonderful.

The hour of the official opening had arrived. The Muhtar rose from his seat and walked to the stage, from where he delivered his speech. "Hoş geldiniz," he cried. "Welcome to you all! This is a very important day for our village. Today we are formally opening our village house. Everybody in our village has worked extremely hard to create this house. We may all be feeling rather exhausted, but even so we're very proud and happy. Nearly everyone, even the women and children, from the eldest to the youngest, has supported this project and done their utmost for the village.

"As you can see, our tradition of working together, in solidarity, has paid off. Thanks to this, we have been able to complete the building of a most beautiful and remarkable house. But we have only been able to achieve this with the help of Güneş and his friends – the Children of the Sun. We have

them to thank for this. It is they who have planned and organized every detail of the work and brought the teams together. They've established a great relationship with the
craftsmen, builders and everyone who's worked on the project. We've all contributed, but the most important help was
provided by our young friends. We would like to express our
gratitude to everyone involved, and to these young people in
particular."

As he concluded his speech, the audience burst into applause,
which continued for what seemed like ages. When it finally
died down, the Governor stepped forward: "This is the first
time in our province," he announced, "that villagers have
constructed a village house entirely by their own efforts,
without receiving help. This is a development that we should
all admire very much indeed. We now look forward to seeing
other villagers benefitting from this example and making
their own village houses, themselves. We'll help those who
want to do this, or other similar activities and we'll provide
them with the necessary support.

"I'd like to take this opportunity to highlight how the importance of the role played by our young people in the revival
of our village, which had been slowly losing its strength and
productivity, has once again come to the fore. For this, I
would like to express my thanks to them. Furthermore, I
would like to share some good news with you: we will be
allocating resources for carrying out infrastructure work for
the village. Even more importantly, I will do everything
within my power to support you and make your village an
example for others."

The Governor's speech was warmly received with a round of
applause. His lending a helping hand in this way was something that nobody had seen for a very long time. It was not
something they'd expected either and was a very positive

move… After the governor had finished, it was the young companions' turn to speak. But what were they planning to say?

It had been decided that Güneş would make a speech on behalf of the Children of the Sun. Slowly and deliberately he walked towards the platform. As he did so, he was wondering what on earth he should say to the villagers and those who had come from other communities. Besides these people, there were others too, including politicians, Muhtars from neighbouring villages, environmentalists and representatives of various NGOs, who would all be listening.

While providing details of the project, he also knew that he should keep his speech brief. Taking a deep breath, he began: "To begin with I would like to say that I hope this village-house will bring good luck and happiness to our village. This is part of a strategic project; one being carried out for the benefit of our village. It is also a socialisation project, one that will end individualisation, the situation where villagers are becoming increasingly isolated from each other, if you like, retiring into their shells. This is a project that will encourage villagers to reunite; come together, work together and have fun together."

His words were met with silence. So, apparently the main issue was some kind of breakdown of the community, of the villagers' social bonds? The young people were right about this; their dream was to get people to come together again, reuniting and reunifying the villagers as a community. They had therefore decided to devote their first project to social solidarity. Güneş took another deep breath: "…Another aim of this project has been to build a typical village house. Unlike most contemporary architecture, the most important feature of traditional village houses is for everything to be designed in accordance with the sun.

96

The building has to face the sun; inside and out of the home there must be sunny spaces for food production and warmth. In spite of this, nowadays, people who carry out restorations are not aware of these hidden qualities. Even more important, this culture of solar architecture must be developed further. This village must be used as an example for every village in our country. This building, the one you see before you, isn't just some ordinary village house. It's a solar house; one heated naturally, without the use of fossil fuels or nuclear energy.

Until now the crowd had remained silent, but then everybody began to clap and cheer. Yes! What they had heard was true. There were houses built according to the Anatolian Sun Culture, although most people didn't know about it. Solar architecture, which was beginning to be used increasingly across the world, had been used in this village since time immemorial. But it was the first time these villagers had become aware of this and it was something they found deeply fascinating. The other intriguing fact they'd learned was that this house, the first to be designed using local culture and built in accordance with "ecological solar architecture," was in their village. This had happened thanks to the thorough research the young friends had made on traditional solar culture, combining it with contemporary developments. This was a source of great joy.

The Governor couldn't resist asking: "How have you managed to capture such high energy efficiency in a village house? Actually, this was an excellent question and one that had a very important answer. Everybody was curious about the secret behind this success. Güneş' reply was relaxed and unhurried: "The secret is that houses used to be designed to make use of the sun. Traditionally, village houses were built using both the sun and underground heat. What we've done is to connect the solar spaces and integrate them with this house. We have renewed and supported the solar system using several new technologies."

Ay glanced at the audience; everybody was listening to Güneş so intently they'd almost forgotten to breathe. Turning back to look at Güneş, she too looked at him differently. "What an impressive guy!" she thought to herself. As indeed he was... Güneş continued to speak and as he did so, he became radiant: it was as if the sun itself had fallen to earth and was talking! Pointing at the roof, Güneş exclaimed. "Look!" he said. "Facing us, you can see only roof tiles. But if you look more closely, you'll notice that there's glass covering the roof. Although it isn't very obvious, the components on the roof are in fact a large sun box. [5]

"The heat that's obtained is stored together with the heat from the ground, which automatically heats the house at night. This system is reversed in summer to cool the building. We have made a passive sun system by covering the front of the çardak with glass. In addition, we have designed and built solar panels and collector pipes that are compatible with the roof architecture and provide electricity and hot water for the house. When there's no sun, the central wood burning stove warms the whole house."

The theory had been explained. Now the time had come to see the system in practice. The Provincial Governor and Ay cut the ribbon together. The young friends then took the

---

[5] *The sun box was first used for the Günsera Project, in Güneşköy, a Sun Village in Ankara. This shape was a model developed for both solar houses and solar greenhouses. (According to this model the glass used in the constructions was a special kind, called solar glass. This type of glass has 90% sun-diffusing capacity. (See the book Günsera, 2012: Ankara.)*

guests around the house and described the village's pioneering sun systems to them.

As the Governor was leaving, he congratulated each of the young companions separately and shook their hands. He asked them to bring the projects that they had designed for the village to his office. It wouldn't be easy. Help given by Governors in the past had not taken projects such as these into account, and the work that'd been done hadn't achieved very much for the village, either. Yet, these youngsters had already started to believe that the ground-breaking projects they wanted to carry out to help the village develop were right.

Divided into groups, they spent the next two days visiting the village houses. Meanwhile, with the help of donations the interior of the house was equipped and opened to the public. The villagers donated various works of art and handicrafts to decorate the village house. Built according to local culture and traditions, the solar house attracted a huge amount of attention, with news of it spreading far afield.

It didn't take long for visitors to show up. Journalists and several TV channels visited what was now being called the Sun Village, which resulted in this unique solar house being acclaimed throughout the country. Interviews were given about the Sun Village and documentaries were made about the house and solar culture. The village became increasingly famous with representatives from the Chamber of Architects, academics from several universities, as well as experts in various fields, coming to see the house. They carried out on-site research studies and surveys. They also asked the Children of the Sun how they could help the village.

Their interest delighted the young companions. But this would not be enough. Getting support from the universities and chamber of architects would also be really important. As the project was unique it would be necessary for them to get new and different opinions and ideas. The suggestions received from the universities and the chamber of architects were discussed, in particular there were talks about holding summer training courses in the village.

With all these offers to help them implement these unique projects, they became increasingly confident. Thanks to the solar house, the village was coming back to life. Some villagers even started to rent out their guest rooms. The Children of the Sun watched these developments with increasing happiness.

It was now time for the second solar phenomenon to hit the village.

Tiny Suns

While Güneş and his friends were sitting talking in the village square, a little boy ran towards them crying "They're here! They're here!" The child stopped and stood there panting; he was completely out of breath. Young Ali was clearly very excited, but the friends wondered why.

"What's happened? Why were you running like that?" Su asked. Again, Ali panted "They're here! They're here!" It was all he could manage to say. Once he'd calmed down a bit, he managed to explain what he'd seen: "The lights. They've come!"

Now everything became clear. The lights they'd ordered had arrived. They all walked to the entrance of the village, where they saw a truck full of lights and lampposts. They spoke with the driver, asking him to take his cargo to the places they'd previously agreed. While Gök rode in the lorry to show him the way, the others sent messages to the team who would be in charge of erecting them. The first light was set up in the square, and the following day was spent erecting the rest at regular intervals around the village. By the evening they were all ready.

As darkness fell, the lights began to twinkle. Twenty lights automatically began to shine simultaneously throughout the village. Everywhere was lit up. Finally, after surviving thousands of years of darkness, a new age of light was dawning in the village. Now the villagers could go out easily at night, do their jobs and pay visits to neighbours and friends after dark.

However, the villagers were curious about how the lights worked, especially as there was no electrical connection involved and no contact between them.

Finally, curiosity got the better of one fellow: "It's very strange," he said. "These lights aren't anything like the ones we're used to." He was looking inquisitively at Güneş and his friends, but as usual Güneş responded with a smile: "Well done for spotting that... From now on, it'll be the sun that lights up our village!" These young people were really strange, first of all they build a solar house and then they start to light the village with solar energy.

Güneş decided it would be a good idea to share a few more details with the villagers. "In our village we'll produce all our own energy. When we spoke with you about development projects, you'll probably remember that lighting for the village was part of the plan. You'll also remember that we decided to use natural sources instead of external ones, such as coal and oil. As you know the important resources for this village are sun, bioenergy, rivers, plants and wood. as it's the easiest and cheapest, we've decided to use solar energy for the lighting."

There was complete silence. Then one of the villagers asked: "How did you find the money?"

It was Gök who replied: "These lights you can see have been donated to our village. A number of companies that produce solar technology heard about our project and told us they were thinking about helping us. Having established contact, we immediately established a close relationship with them."

Su spoke up: "We wanted to get lights that were in keeping with the village architecture. Our dear friend, Ay, designed a special light for our village. One of the companies liked her design very much and offered to produce them without taking the patent, which we still have rights over. So, subject to a few conditions, we accepted their offer. The lights you're looking at now were therefore made exclusively for our village, thanks to Ay who designed them and the company who made them.

Doğa felt she needed to give more details: "Yes... Our friend, Ay, donated her rights for the design to the village. As these lights are being sold, the money coming from the patent will provide income for our Village Development Fund."

The villagers were deeply affected by these words. They looked at each other, then back at Ay. She could see a look of gratitude in their faces. "Well done Ay! Three cheers for Ay," they cried, cheering her loudly. Their sincerity moved Ay; for her, this definitely made it worth the effort.

One of the young men's curiosity got the better of him: "We love you very much, we really do, and we want to thank you for everything you've done. But... we were wondering why this design is so different from all the others we've seen. Do they have a different function?" "I looked at the light designs that would meet the needs of our village," replied Ay, "but I didn't like them. I thought the solar batteries and accumulators used for storing energy were really ugly. I began to wonder if it would be possible to make better ones and drafted a design for this one. The model you're seeing now is the result. I hope you like it."

In response to this, a middle-aged man in the crowd said: "I've seen solar energy lights before. They've all got panels and accumulators. But in your model, I can't see them. Yours are much more beautiful and simpler. And what's more, *they look just like tiny suns*!" "Hey! That's wonderful. Thank you so much for your kind remarks," replied Ay. "You're absolutely right. My idea was to make the lights look like tiny suns lighting up our nights and, in the end, I came up with this model, which takes into account features of the sun it-self."

Following Ay's speech, everybody looked more carefully at the lights. They definitely did look like real suns but on a miniature scale: tiny suns suspended in the air, lighting the darkness. The villagers realized that for the first time they had come face to face with a real artist.

That night the villagers saw Aykız, and she looked as beau-tiful as a fairy. Holding the sun in her hands, the Aykız flew out of the night sky towards them, reaching out with a light that was illuminating their dark world.

Chapter 5

Tiny suns

Stones that absorb the Sun's energy

During May there were some major developments in the village. One of the Governor's officials contacted the youngsters to ask what infrastructure they thought would be suitable for the Sun Village and to share their suggestions. The Governor also promised to help at the opening. Not wanting to miss out on this opportunity, they knew they had to act promptly. So, they prepared the projects without delay and sent them to the Governor.

Not long after, it was agreed that the Governor would finance half the anticipated budget and this money would be added to the village funds. At last, the groundwork for the village could begin. However, since the budget was limited, the youngsters faced some serious concerns for which they had to find cost-effective solutions. If this didn't happen, the work couldn't be completed and that would mean postponing everything until the following year.

The youngsters began to discuss these issues at length. How could the infrastructure of the Sun Village they dreamed about ever become a reality? They knew that nothing else would inspire them in quite the same way, so once again they would have to do the work themselves. First, the infrastructure would have to have all the necessary sanitary provisions and in no way should the natural ecological structure of the village be harmed, as it dated back to ancient times. But how could they achieve this?

So that they could benefit from previous village traditions, they decided to investigate. Although the village had no sewage system, as such, there were washing and toilet facilities and these were natural systems that didn't produce any damaging environmental waste. Instead, all the natural waste was converted for reuse in the village. Why couldn't they use a system like this? Why shouldn't it be developed and become a model for use in other villages too? After all, this was a natural system that had been used for hundreds of years.

It was also known that, at one time, Anatolia had benefitted from some very advanced privies, including Hittite, Greek, Roman, Seljuk and Ottoman systems, as well as some even more advanced ones that had been used over thousands of years. At a time when there still were no hygienic toilet facilities in the west, the Anatolian lavatory was already pretty advanced. Some of the most well-known examples were the public privies in the ancient city of Ephesus, and later the marble latrines developed by the architect Sinan, for use in mosques, inns and bath houses, together, all of which had some artistic features. These were usually squat privies; more commonly known as *alla Turca* toilets.

Village privies were a simple and basic style of the squat toilet. Still in use today, these privies have both ecological and economical features. Separate from the home, they are spartan structures made of wood, which are usually built on a raised part of the garden.

What's more, paper, as well as artificial and harmful cleaners, such as detergents, are never used. Together with the solid waste, the water used for washing flows into a cesspit, or soakaway. The resulting compost is used to nourish the garden's vegetable patch and fruit trees, while the water that accumulates in these pits eventually seeps back into the soil. In this way, both the waste and wastewater are reused on the land. With this system, the waste does not pollute the environment and energy is not consumed. On the contrary, over time it transforms into a useful product and is a system that has many economic and ecological advantages over sewage systems, which not only pollute the environment but are also very expensive to operate.

The youngsters decided to reintroduce the village toilet system. They made the first example and when the villagers saw how hygienic this innovative version of the original was, they liked it so much most of them followed suit for their own facilities.

The time had now come to repair the village's water system. With help from one of the Governor's assistants, the iron pipes, which had resulted in various illnesses, were changed and replaced with a healthier system. In the early weeks of May, after the work on the infrastructure had been completed - and at remarkable speed - the Children of the Sun thought it was time to start on the tasks that would make the village even more beautiful.

Gök, whose main interests lay in the infrastructural work, briefly explained what needed to be done: "Listen," he said. "One of the most important things we need to do is to restore the village to its former glory. The roads and streets are completely wrecked and some of the buildings are too, and what's left are in ruins. All these should be rebuilt, urgently. To start with, the roads and streets must be restored, then the ruined buildings. I also think we need to thoroughly clean up the environment."

Everyone was in total agreement. They could use some of the money invested in the infrastructure fund to tidy up the village. All the tractor and the truck drivers got to work. They gathered the stone, wood and other useful materials from the ruined houses and stored it in a place just outside the village, so it could be used later.

The time had now come to remake the village's streets and squares.

The Children of the Sun had gathered in a garden, for tea and a chat. They were all exhausted, but they knew that as long as they were doing something useful, they would be able to overcome their fatigue and keep going. The majority of the villagers were keen for the streets to be surfaced with asphalt or concrete, but the youngsters didn't agree with this idea. They knew that the streets were the arteries, the lifeblood of the village, and it wouldn't be right to make a decision without considering the consequences. Su was the first to speak. "Roads are one of the most important aspects of village life. We must ensure that we bring the street culture back to life, otherwise we can't protect the village's traditional customs."

Before Güneş could say anything, Ay said: "Even though these days they're neglected, the roads, garden walls, and houses still lend an aesthetic, visually appealing look to the streets."

"Hang on a minute," said Güneş. "As far as the plan for the streets and squares is concerned, what we'll use to make them is really important in terms of the villagers' wellbeing. It could be that the local authority and village management don't know about this, or perhaps they just think it's easier and cheaper, but their usual way is to pour cement on the roads or cover them with asphalt. Most likely, they're unaware that using all this stuff on the roads has an incredibly negative impact on the environment and using massive amounts of concrete adversely affects the climate. For example, in the summer, concrete can make towns and cities unbearably hot."

He saw that his friends were hanging on his every word, and the passion of his voice increased: "If we really care about all this, the roads in the village centre and the garden walls that edge them need to be made with a special stone, called granite. In this way, the climate in the central part of the village will be balanced, making it more comfortable for the people who live there.

Granite is really important, chiefly because it isn't harmful to people's health. Granite absorbs the sun's rays and using it on roads prevents them from becoming overheated in the summer. In the same way, during the winter months, this stone also creates a warmer environment, as it naturally absorbs energy. Perhaps one of granite's most important features is that, in the winter, when the weather is extremely cold, it causes the ice and the snow to melt more quickly. We could describe granite as *the stone that absorbs the sun's energy*. It's definitely the best material for us to use."

Agreeing with him, Gök said: "Friends, as I think you're all aware of how critical the situation is, you'll all agree that we should be using granite to repair the ruined walls and to resurface the streets and squares. Doing it like this will be important for how the village looks too. In the old days, the streets were paved with granite that was excavated from a nearby stone quarry. If we can use the same stone to make it like it was before, it'll also mean that we won't have to spend so much money buying other materials."

Everyone was of the same mind and immediately explained the situation to the villagers. Even though they had until then preferred the idea of using concrete or asphalt when they understood the reasons why granite was so essential, the villagers, for the most part, agreed with this decision.

All the same, some continued to object, insisting that asphalt should be used instead. In spite of this, they fell silent once they were told that the decision had been made and the project agreed.

In the days that followed, the stone quarry was reopened, and work started. The cut granite was transported to selected parts of the village and as funds were limited, the villagers chose to do the work themselves. Divided into five separate work crews, they began working simultaneously and in what seemed like no time at all, the roads were paved, and the walls repaired.

Back in the city, the Governor heard about their endeavours. Curious to learn what they'd been doing, he paid an unexpected visit to the village, accompanied by his assistants. They were all very surprised when they saw what had been achieved. The once ruined village now looked clean, tidy and picturesque. It had become a place that was really worth seeing. Where once there was nothing more than ruins, the village now looked as if it had been born again from the depths of history.

The Governor very much liked what he saw. He warmly congratulated the Children of the Sun and the villagers: "We've been telling you for ages that you should protect your village and preserve our culture but until now no one had followed our advice or acted on our suggestions. What you've done is incredibly important. Your work not only looks good, it's all of excellent quality. It's so good it can become an example for other villages too. I thank you all, most sincerely." As he was leaving the village, the Governor was smiling broadly. This was because he had finally found the solution for which he had long been searching.

With the help of these youngsters and by sending one to each district in the region, they could begin to create villages that were in-keeping with the culture. Meanwhile, the villagers would never forget the words Güneş had used to describe granite: *"stones that absorb the sun's energy."*

A workshop

The village had another event to look forward to, and today it was one everyone was really excited about. Important visitors were coming, and meetings would be held at which the future of the village would be discussed. Preparations for these meetings, which they were calling a workshop, had begun several days earlier.

As the time for the meetings approached, there was a flurry of activity in the village. As on previous occasions, the square was prepared: chairs were brought from homes and a platform and sound system was set up. Likewise, cauldrons were brought out and preparations were made to cook some of the village's favourite traditional dishes.

Many visits had already been made to the village and various activities had taken place; however, this workshop was going to be a much more significant event. To begin with, many academics would be coming to the workshop from universities in Ankara, including METU, as well as from other universities. Furthermore, representatives from various governmental and non-governmental organizations would also be taking part.

As well as those invited, almost everyone from the village was also in the square in which the workshop would take place. The villagers were chatting quietly amongst themselves. They were all in a high state of excitement, as the subject of discussion would be about the village and its future.

First, the village Muhtar and a lecturer called Metin Bey, took their place on the platform, followed by Güneş and the rest of the speakers. Among the ten speakers, were experts in their fields, including planners, architects, sociologists, anthropologists and artists. When the Muhtar stood up to make the first talk you could have cut the silence like a knife. Everyone's interest was focused on him.

Before getting down to the main business of the day, the Muhtar began by thanking everyone for coming to the workshop: "Today is a very important day for our village. For the first time ever in Turkey, we're coming together with university academics as part of a joint initiative. Together we'll start by discussing our village in particular and then the problems faced by Turkish villagers in general. What can be done for our villages that are increasingly in decline; losing their character and even disappearing altogether? What can we do to revive them? We will be hearing about all this and more from our esteemed guests. With these words, I would like to hand over the stage to the experts…"

He turned to Metin Bey and extending his hand, said: "If you please, Metin Bey, we're all, ready to listen to you." Metin Bey gave courses on the sun at university level and was one of Turkey's most renowned planners. Also known as the Sun Hoca, he accepted the role of chair. Highly experienced, he was responsible for the academic programme and preliminary preparations and was in contact with the other academics. His work on Anatolian solar cultures attracted much interest and his reputation extended way beyond Turkey's shores. He'd already written and published fifteen books on the subject.

Thanking the Muhtar and everyone else taking part, he began his speech by saying that he was very happy to be there: "First of all, I would like to congratulate the village and our young friends who prepared the project. With it they have addressed an important shortcoming in our young Republic

113

that has been ignored up until now; that is, the village development project. This is a courageous enterprise and one I celebrate in its entirety.

"The Village Development Project was one of the Republic's most significant programmes... In keeping with the project, an example of a model republican village was created, and plans were made. *Köy Enstitüleri* - Village Institutes - were established for the educational infrastructure: Community Centres – *Halk Evleri* – were opened for the benefit of villagers, while Community Halls – *Halk Odaları* – were opened in rural areas. Unfortunately, as always, internal and external forces undermined these efforts. The institutes were closed; village education has been brought to a complete impasse.

"The *Halk Evleri* and *Halk Odaları* were also closed down, and with this the enlightenment of Anatolia was cut short. Now, you, the villagers are trying to deal with these consequences, while trying to determine the real and true aim of the republic, to "start the development from the village," in an extremely restricted and very difficult situation. I can't congratulate you enough. I think it's fair to say that this is actually a project of the Republic and that it will become a good example for every institution in our country; one that everyone should take into account and contribute towards."

These last words caused a profound silence among the spectators. The villagers found what had been said absolutely fascinating. No one had ever shared things like this with them before, but now they were really listening. Looking intently at his audience, Metin Bey decided he should explain the meaning of the project to them more clearly: "I want to tell you a simple truth that perhaps you don't realise: you are heirs to an Anatolian Village Culture that is ten thousand years old."

Another shock wave engulfed the community. This was certainly a different perspective and one they rather enjoyed hearing but even so, it was the first time they'd heard of such a thing. So, was he telling the truth, or could he be exaggerating? Their feelings of curiosity intensified. Pleased with the effect his words were having, Metin Bey continued: "In order to attain this level of cultural know-how, Anatolian towns and villages have been developing for thousands of years. Today, everything, which has a true understanding of modern culture and hasn't been spoiled, bears traces of this rich culture.

"The unique feature of this culture is that it's based on the sun. It's because of this that we've given it the name, *sun culture*. Today you are living with the sun, in a village shaped by the sun. You're living in houses that bear the traces of solar architecture and feed yourselves with food produced with the help of the sun. You are living in harmony with the sun. And among all the cultures of the world, this one has significant value."

Few remained unaffected by these words. The villagers were not aware that they were living in a village with a sun culture. It was the first time they'd heard that their culture was so important. Metin Bey highlighted another truth, too: "With the widespread use of petroleum and nuclear energy, the sun culture has been deliberately discouraged, even deliberately disabled. A world where cartels dominate has been created to exploit these energy sources. It is because of this that the sun culture has gradually disappeared. Modern civilization, based on fossil fuels and nuclear energy, pollutes the world and has negatively impacted on all living things."

The audience before him looked so stunned, it was as if they had been turned to stone. "This is why the sun has begun to regain its importance in the world." He continued. "Now solar technology is being developed again and solar power plants are being established. Cities based on solar energy are being built and solar architecture is becoming quite common. But regrettably, despite all these developments there is a big deficiency in terms of sun culture. I want to make it perfectly clear that in this new world, it is the villages of Anatolia that suffer the most. This is because this culture of 'living in harmony with the sun' should be even more a characteristic of rural life."

These villagers had not known how important and necessary the sun culture was for the world. That is to say, previous generations who had lived on this land knew the sun much better and had made it an integral part of their lives, creating a solar culture in the process. But even so, some self-serving cliques were managing to successfully ensure that this culture would become a thing of the past...

Now everybody understood how much these forgotten cultures were needed, not only for villages but for the whole world. They were so happy that this culture had its origins in their village life. They just wondered if it really could be true. Of course, it was true... After all, these words were being spoken by a famous professor!

Following on from Metin Bey, several university academics spoke about the importance of the philanthropic and productive life culture of the village and the importance of women in rural culture. Another spokes about biodiversity, and the plants and animal species in the region. Yet another gave a talk about how various natural materials were used in different areas and the culture relating to it. Anthropologists and sociologists covered topics, such as the richness of village culture, from various perspectives, providing some important information that the villagers had not previously heard.

116

They explained about other parts of the world too, in terms of the preservation and development of village culture, giving details of some successful projects by way of example. They emphasized the importance of ecology, natural life and art in village culture. By the end of the workshop, it was clear that almost everybody had the same idea about revitalising the sun culture and the development and protection of village culture in the Caucasian region of Anatolia. It was certainly proving to be a very successful and productive workshop.

After these informative talks, several state officials spoke about other projects being implemented in the region. Delegates from non-governmental organizations pledged to cooperate with issues such as the protection of natural resources and the implementation phase of the project. The experts had spoken first, and their talks had exceeded expectations, providing some very interesting food for thought, and the time had now come for the villagers to speak.

But first there was the lunchbreak. Everyone said they thoroughly enjoyed the traditional dishes, which had been prepared and cooked by women from the village. Afterwards the workshop got underway again with Metin Bey asking for the villagers' opinions and those of them who wished to speak did so. They said that they had liked what the academics had said and shared their own ideas about village culture and its development.

After that, the discussion turned to village art. Three young women put on an impromptu performance about the tradition of requesting a girl's hand in marriage. During their interpretation, they sang folk songs and recited Turkish poetry, which everyone thoroughly enjoyed.

Metin Bey expressed his thanks to all the contributors, saying that the workshop had been a complete success. Before concluding the workshop, he summarised the main points and handed the notes he'd made to the Muhtar. He also said that he would prepare a report on the workshop, which he would send to the village. He ended with these words: "Never forget that these projects are yours. You are the ones who will be bringing them to life and putting them into practice. Don't forget that. *Şimdiden başarılar*, I know it'll be a success!"

In the course of the workshop the villagers had learned just how important their village culture was, not just locally and nationally but internationally, and from this they concluded that something so incredibly valuable would certainly need to be protected.

Guests

Soon the whole country heard the news about the workshop. This led to the village becoming increasingly recognised by the public and visitors began to turn up, curious to see for themselves what the villagers had achieved. Güneş and his friends took responsibility for managing the village house. There was a small kitchen at the back with cooking facilities. They began to serve tea, coffee and sandwiches; however, the youngsters were not satisfied with this and took the decision to build a solar cooker and solar oven as soon as possible.

On arrival, people would usually come straight to the village house, where they'd meet and chat with the Children of the Sun. In accordance with village tradition, no money was requested for tea and coffee. The subject of most interest to outsiders was the village's sun culture and, in an attempt to learn more about it, they asked a variety of questions. Among these visitors were people who had left the village but wanted to take a closer look at what was going on. There were even people choosing to spend their holidays in the village.

The former villagers, now city dwellers, were bewildered by what they saw on their return. The grim old village had gone and, in its place, there now was idyllic one. None of them could believe that the village had been able to change so much in a such a short space of time. The increasing number of sightseers began to cause accommodation problems for the village. To resolve these difficulties, Su and Doğa visited the householders one by one to determine which homes would meet the necessary standards for guests.

All the village houses were two storeys. Families usually lived on the lower floors, rarely using the upper ones, which is where the guest rooms were. Su and Doğa spoke with the villagers and checked which rooms would be suitable. They eventually identified around twenty rooms. The youngsters made a list, which they displayed in the village house. On arrival guests were provided with the appropriate accommodation, according to this list. In this way, the contributions from the guests also provided income for the village.

Some people suggested an ecotourism project, as way of boosting income for the village. But this would prove to be difficult, if not impossible, as most were unfamiliar with such a concept. For the villagers, especially the elderly, is would be virtually impossible to teach them the do's and don'ts of eco-tourism and expect them to put them into practice. Moreover, the tourism infrastructure of the village was not yet ready for this, so they decided to shelve this idea, at least for the time being.

Güneş and his friends continued to pursue their investigations across all these different areas. They held a meeting with the former villagers who'd come to visit. They asked for their help with renovating the old houses, to ensure that they'd be in keeping with the original ones. At least they would be able to renovate their own houses themselves. Three, two from outside the village, said they would like to renovate their houses but weren't able to, as they couldn't stay in the village.

Güneş was able to persuade them, by suggesting that the houses could be renovated using his team, but they would need to meet the expenses themselves. In this way, the houses could be repaired and the craftsmen and young people working on them wouldn't be left idle. In addition, the houses could be rented, which would provide an income. The sums required were paid into the village fund, and the renovation work began at once.

The young companions devised the projects, and renovation teams worked on the buildings. As the same repair methods were being applied in each case, their work was becoming much easier. More solar systems were being added and everyone had a sense of pride in building houses based on Anatolian sun culture.

At long last, the state gave its approval for the solar roof systems and agreed to provide incentives. Even so, no effort has been forthcoming in the application of the sun culture in people's homes. The Children of the Sun, on the other hand, were very much aware that they were working on exemplary projects for authentic solar houses.

By midsummer, two more of the old houses had been repaired and with these the number of beds available increased. As a result, the number of visitors also grew. The village was galvanized by all this and its economy was thriving. Ecological lifestyles were becoming widespread. Day by day, the hopes and dreams of the Children of the Sun were intensifying.

The biggest surprise happened at the beginning of August...

Summer School

There was a huge commotion in the village square. Everybody was talking nineteen to the dozen. The main topic of conversation seemed to be trying to find out what the Children of the Sun were planning to do. Amidst this confusion, Güneş took his place on the platform and asked for silence. The Muhtar came to stand next to him and everyone saw that they were both holding sheets of paper in their hands. Güneş began to read a list of students' names, followed by the Muhtar, who read out the names of the house owners with whom they would be staying.

As the students' names were called, they met up with the people with whom they'd be staying and accompanied them to their homes. Within half an hour, the village square was almost empty. The only people to stay behind were the Children of the Sun and some teachers. The teachers would be staying at the Village House. Shortly afterwards, no one apart from a few visitors remained in the village square.

A group of new visitors were wandering around the village in complete astonishment. First, two buses had arrived full of young people. Then the square had been full to bursting with villagers and students. Before long the square had been abuzz with activity. One of the visitors took it upon themselves to ask a villager what was going on: "What's happening?" they enquired. "We don't understand what's going on." The villager replied with some pride: "They're university students. They're here as our guests and they've come to help us with the village museum."

The reason why the village was facing such a big event was connected with a statement made by the university teacher, Metin Bey. Following the workshop, he had immediately contacted various university departments, including architecture, ethnology, sociology and landscape architecture, to suggest that one of their summer schools could be held at the newly established Sun Village. The university authorities gave their approval immediately. They even managed to find the resources to cover travel expenses, accommodation and catering costs. First to arrive in the village were the students and the younger academics, who came together in vehicles rented by the university's local trade associations.

This made all the villagers very cheerful, particularly the Muhtar and they decided to welcome them in the best way possible. At first, it was thought that it would be difficult for so many people to stay in the village at the same time. This problem was shared with the villagers, who were asked to help. The villagers were very responsive and came one by one to say they could accommodate a guest and, in no time at all, it became clear that there was more than enough accommodation for a hundred guests. It was almost as if the villagers were competing with each other.

As well as enjoyable, summer schools were considered to be a highly beneficial activity for the students. It would be their first opportunity to put the knowledge they had acquired into practice. This was why they were all looking forward to it so much. Working with the university teachers, the Children of the Sun had identified what needed to be done in the village and developed a work programme. By the time the students arrived in the village, the working environment was ready. The only problem that remained was with whom each student would stay. Fortunately, this problem was easily solved.

Then it was time to decide on some regulations for the summer school.

The students came from different academic fields. Their work would be multidisciplinary, both in their own areas of study, as well as in other fields. Before they began their field-work, the students would have to attend an induction pro-gramme to bring them all up to speed. To prepare the pro-gramme, the teachers came together with the Children of the Sun in the garden of the village house.

For this they would have to work for three days. On the first day, Güneş and his friends explained the village project and on the following two the teachers provided information on Anatolian village folk culture, authentic building restoration, village life and organization, the village economy, and rural settlements and their features. Now, the working groups could be created.

Meanwhile, the students who were staying with families spent the morning having breakfast with their hosts and mak-ing the most of being in a village home. They examined and sketched the architecture and also assessed the houses in cul-tural terms, so they could add this information to their study projects. Staying with village families created a warm atmos-phere and sense of intimacy for the students and renowned Anatolian hospitality was clear for all to see.

Older villagers in particular treated the students as if they were their children. The young people were not unresponsive to this affection and strong ties developed between the stu-dents and the villagers. In the end everyone felt as if they were part of a big family... sharing laughter and sometimes a few tears. In the evenings, the students would get together to share their experiences with their friends, and in this way a consensus began to form.

When they'd first arrived at the village, they'd thought that the villagers were, in their own way, somewhat aloof and reserved. Before they came, some had even imagined that villagers were ignorant and rather uncouth. In spite of this, as they got to know the village and the villagers, their thoughts and feelings began to change.

Coming from the city, the students were having a hard time doing many of the jobs the young villagers could do. It became clear that while they themselves had a great deal of knowledge, much of it was irrelevant when it came to everyday life. The villagers on the other hand had all the practical skills and knowledge required and when the time came, they could apply this local knowledge in the best way possible. All the villagers knew about farming and animal husbandry, and what they didn't know they'd learnt about at 'the university of life.'

Maybe, these villagers didn't know anything about plant species in Indonesia, for example, but the fact remained that they could identify virtually every plant and animal that lived in their region and they also knew how to make the most them. The young villagers knew a great deal about botany too, more than most biology students, and certainly their practical knowledge of construction was way more than that of the architecture students.

The college girls felt pretty embarrassed when they learnt what girls and women in the village were capable of doing. Every young woman in the village knew how to produce foodstuffs and when it came to meals, they were all talented cooks. They were happy to teach their culinary skills to those students who asked. The students were equally amazed when they saw the young women's sewing, lacemaking and embroidery skills. It's fair to say, the village women had all been raised to be talented artists.

For the first time in their lives, the young students recognised the cultural wealth of Anatolian villages and they weren't able to hide their admiration. Although the architecture students had read numerous books and examined hundreds of buildings during their studies, they had never seen village architecture: for example, the fine detail of the carved wooden walls and ceilings, so much part of the rural style. Here they were seeing village architectural design and, amazed by the expertise they saw, found it impossible not to be affected by them.

Despite the normally intense heat of August, as it was surrounded by woods and forests and the squares were covered by vines, it didn't feel too hot in the village. There were shady places nearly everywhere, so no one became overwhelmed by heat while outside. Also, the breezes coming from the mountain that blew through the valleys dissipated the heat and made it feel pleasantly cooler; rather like natural air conditioning...

The solar spaces in the village houses in which they were staying simply astonished the architecture students. These places appeared to be able to cool or warm the interiors. It was also evident that these were arranged to make domestic chores much more comfortable. But what surprised them most were the rooms. Decorated with traditional furnishings, these were even more beautiful and comfortable than rooms in a five-star hotel. Almost like individual entities, each one had everything a family could need.

In the rooms there were hearths decorated with carved wood, divans covered with colourful kilims, carpets and small rugs on the floor, delicately carved ceilings, reliefs showing figures of the stars and the sun of the most exceptional beauty. Almost reaching to ceiling height were carved wooden shelves that ran the length of the room, on which household goods, including handmade copper pots, pans and jugs, were stored, adding a different kind of opulence to the living space.

On entering the rooms, there were cupboards that ran the length of one wall. Embellished with carvings, these wooden doors opened onto another treasure-trove. In the middle was the largest of these, where the quilts and bedrolls were kept. Immediately below these rooms was the byer where provisions were stored. One of the other doors opened onto a small closet containing washing facilities while, behind another door, were the things needed for everyday life.

So, within these rooms there was everything a family could possibly require, all in one compact space. They could warm themselves by the stove; cook whatever food they wanted and eat it from the *sofra*; entertain their neighbours or invite them over for refreshments and relax and go to sleep in their beds.

These young people, particularly those who were stuck behind four concrete walls in the big cities, in featureless, dysfunctional and totally impersonal rooms, and who didn't have the faintest idea about village life and culture, were truly astounded by this dazzling array and it's no exaggeration to say, they were extremely impressed.

The things that they were seeing in an average village house were much more precious and beautiful than anything they'd seen in the most luxurious hotel [6] and the Summer School

---

[6] *The village rooms mentioned in the story were chosen as examples from a project carried out in   Ürünlü village: the Ürünlü cultural village project.*

students were actually staying in *these* rooms. There were however other things that surprised them too…

A few days after they'd settled in, two female students were sipping tea and chatting with their hosts in the çardak. One of the girls, called Selin, had noticed how fresh the rooms smelled, and was curious: "The room we're staying in always smells so wonderful. I wonder if you've put something in it without us realising," she asked.

Musa, the host's son, explained on behalf of his mother: "No, we never go in your room. The smell is from the materials used when this house was built." Çiğdem, Selin's friend, immediately responded: "So, did you add some kind of fragrance to the materials you used when you were building the room?" This question raised a gentle laugh from the family. "No," Musa replied, still smiling, "We haven't added any fragrance. They're already fragrant, as we use a special kind of tree to make our buildings. It's a resinous timber, which will always smell like this. What's more, it's brilliant for keeping away any harmful pests, too."

It was the first time the girls had heard of such a thing. Suddenly, Selin thought of a question: "Since I came here, I've been sleeping really well. At night I've been sleeping like a log and when I wake up in the morning, I feel great. Do you have any idea why?" Çiğdem had a question to ask too: "Do you know, I've suffered from asthma since I was born. But I've been breathing well since the day I arrived. It's like I never had asthma. But so far, I haven't been able to work out why."

Now, it was Musa's father who replied: "There are a few things that make the rooms much healthier, things we pay a lot of attention to. As Musa told you, the resinous trees we use are carefully selected. We also cover the walls with a mud mixture, to which we add fragrant herbs, such as mint and thyme. Therefore, not only do our rooms smell wonderful, they help with our breathing too. They also help to get rid of germs that can make us ill. Besides this, constantly having the range lit ventilates the room, and the air constantly changes, circulates, if you like. This and similar methods have been used for many centuries. The ones I've mentioned are just a few examples. As nobody knows about these methods anymore, they're not being used in modern concrete buildings."

Selin and Çiğdem, both architectural students, were more than a little astonished by these words. They had never heard about this culture, or these kinds of materials being used in modern buildings. On the other hand, nearly everyone in the village knew so much about this kind of construction. They knew about stone and brickwork, mortar and plaster. They also knew how to equip their homes with healthy systems.

During their stay in the village, Selin and Çiğdem learnt many new things about village culture. Later they would be given the opportunity to put what they'd learned into practice in the buildings they made with the village craftsmen and young construction teams.

On leaving the village, they decided not to carry out any more building projects until they'd examined Anatolian architectural culture in detail. This decision would eventually be the principal theme of their future careers.

The highlands

The students were working a half-day, which gave them plenty of free time for both business and pleasure. After their routine daily tasks, they would explore the surrounding countryside, often accompanied by some of the villagers. On these trips they discovered some very interesting places. They plunged headlong into the dark forests and crept into secret caves. They swam in ice-cold streams and caught trout...

This countryside was so rich that wherever and whenever they went, they encountered more and more beauty and fascinating things.

The expeditions they made with the Children of the Sun were really interesting, too. A particular one, which the young people would never forget, was a tour of the Dark Forest. Their starting point was the village square. The expedition would last all day, so everybody brought along a packed lunch. They were accompanied by a forest engineer, who had worked in the forest for many years.

An experienced and a skilled observer, as they walked, he told them about the mysterious world of the forest. The more unknown secrets he revealed about the trees, and the surprising relationships between the plants and animals, the more amazed these urban youngsters became. They felt as if they were in a different world and almost as if they were on a different planet. It was as if they had become lost in the unnatural life of the city, while now the nature they were seeing was full of infinite beauty and riches.

Around the same time, the students had planned an expedition to the *yayla* – the highland pastures. A German professor, who was researching Anatolian Culture, also wanted to come along. He said he'd never been to the Anatolian highlands before and insisted on joining them. Some had objected to his coming along, as they didn't want him to know about the unique character of the highlands but Güneş and his friends did not consider his joining the expedition to be a risk.

The group set off early. Trekking through the forest, and fording rivers, finally they passed through the Dark Forest, before arriving on the yayla. There were highland dwellings located on the rugged terrain between the edge of the forest and the beginning of the highland pastures. The buildings took the form of small wooden huts raised on short stakes. How lovely these tiny houses looked, dotted across the landscape.

Keeping to the narrow pathways, the youngsters visited some of these huts. They examined them inside and out. They drank cold, fresh water from the nearby streams. A few students made sketches of the dwellings. Finally, everyone spread out on the grass to eat the food that they'd brought with them and relax.

Then it was time to learn about the highlands. They wondered what could be the main reason for building this type of hut. What did people do here? What did they eat or drink while they were here? How had they managed to survive in this area, so close to the forest, especially as there were wild animals?

These were the type of questions the youngsters thought about as they were sitting on the grass and they started to ask all kinds of questions that sprang to mind. Güneş and his friends, as well as the few villagers who'd accompanied them, were listening to them patiently. It didn't take long for it to become obvious that the students didn't have the faintest ideas about the culture of the yayla and that it would be necessary to tell them about it.

After they had finished asking their questions, Güneş stood up and looked at the faces around him. He was surprised that the youngsters knew absolutely nothing about yayla traditions, which had continued for thousands of years. In fact, he had not expected them to be so alienated from this culture and was sorry that this was the case.

Having composed his thoughts, finally he began to speak: "Our yayla – our highland pastures – are a vital part of rural life. Each village has their own highland area and local people go up to their own special part of the yayla every year. Some people stay there for two, sometimes three months. They go to the yayla at the start of every summer and when the weather turns cooler, they return to their villages.

"This area, where they stay, is at an altitude of more than two- thousand metres. While our friends are sweltering on the coasts, these people are feeling the chilly mountain breezes." Feeling those same chilly breezes themselves, some of the students wrapped themselves in the blankets they had bought from the village before settling down again to listen to Güneş and his friends.

One raised his hand: "Could you explain why the highland pastures – the yayla – is so necessary?" Güneş paused, only glancing briefly at the questioner to acknowledge his presence, before continuing. He would be dealing with this subject later on: "The yayla is a vital part of Anatolian culture. It's a really important aspect of our living culture. Just think, it's one that's developed over thousands of years." He paused for a moment for this to sink in.

"Anatolia is essential for food production and a large proportion of the villagers' winter provisions are produced in these highlands during the summer months. Almost every villager has either small or large livestock. These animals feed on grass and the multitude of plants and flowers that grow in these mountain pastures. The milk from these animals is rich and full, and the cheese, yogurt and butter they make is completely natural and full of unique and exceptional flavours. What's more, there's nowhere else where you can find meat of the quality that comes from the animals that have grazed on these highland pastures. It's absolutely delicious.

"The villagers get all their meat and milk products from these animals. Another thing is, the diversity of the plants, herbs and flowers that grow here make this an ideal area for producing a very special and fragrant honey. There's also an abundance of fruits, berries and medicinal herbs on this mountain. The plants that grow here are completely natural and organic. It's well known that some of the most precious natural remedies produced in Anatolia are made using these plants." Güneş looked at the young boy who had earlier asked the question: the young boy caught his eye and without saying another word, lowered his gaze.

How could a person become so alienated from his own culture?

Meanwhile, Çiğdem wondered how people were able to survive on the highlands. For example, what did they eat and drink? This time, it was Musa who answered. "On the highlands, people usually eat a lot of the animal products, such as cheese, yogurt, butter and milk. There is a wide range of dishes unique to the yayla, many of which are dairy based. Also, up here there are plants, herbs, nuts, mushrooms and vegetables to eat. All of which are delicious, fresh, healthy and full of natural goodness."

Musa's explanation made the students think twice about the food they usually ate. The food they ate in cities; the fast food, the chemicals in the milk, yogurt, tinned foods… and what about all that coloured, additive filled liquid called 'fruit juice', but which doesn't contain any actual fruit? Their unease and remorse showed clearly in their faces. They began to feel as if they'd been deceived. That is to say, they now realised how disconnected their diet and their lifestyles were from Anatolia's natural world and culture.

They were positively ashamed of having become so estranged from their own land and traditions.

A young man, who obviously thought that having a good time was essential, couldn't resist asking: "How *can* you possibly live up here for three months without anything to do? I mean, no fun, no entertainment?" He was of course referring to bars, discos and pop music. Musa thought for a moment before replying. "Look!" he said. "Look how rich our village is! We have our own unique *türkü* folk songs, poetry, *mani* and folk dances. It's these that reflect our real values." The young students were doing their best to understand what Musa was telling them. Instead of complaining, or imitating others, the villagers created their own entertainment. Now, that beats it all…

Another student was curious to learn something but was slightly embarrassed to ask. He finally summoned the courage: "But how and where do you have fun when you're up here in the yayla?" Aygün, a singer and *saz* player in the village, was able to give him a simple explanation: "Why, every night we light a fire, and people can come and join us if they like. We sit round the fire, chatting and sharing our problems. Sometimes, at the weekend, we really have fun. The weekends are the time when we get together to sing songs, tell tales, dance, and musicians come to play. It's a great way to unwind and get rid of the week's stress!"

As she looked into the faces around her, she realised they were all hanging on her every word: "And, by the way, our *Şenlik* – our highland festivals – they're *really* famous. Every year, we meet up with our neighbours from other yayla villages. On that day, we get together to celebrate the Sun Bayram. We set off in the dark, before sunrise. We meet at the top of this mountain, pray together and make a sacrifice. Then we cook rice dishes, eat and drink and make merry: people play the saz, while others sing and dance. We also hold different events, such as bull wrestling and oil wrestling, saz competitions and recitations. We award prizes. All this symbolises our merrymaking, a culture which has been celebrated since time immemorial and one that still continues today. These Sun Bayrams are celebrations that embody our delight and passion about being part of nature and rebirth."

The students were utterly astonished. They now remembered the importance of the sun, of nature; things that they'd totally forgotten. According to them, the sun was a distant star, something far away and nature was the plants they saw growing around them, and the trees! But now it was becoming clear to them that these villagers thought differently about such things. They knew all about the sun and nature and how essential they were for life, much more than the students did. They continued to celebrate such things at feasts and festivals and were doing everything they could to pass their traditions from one generation to the next.

But unfortunately, nowadays it seemed that any appreciation of these things had been forgotten. Nonetheless, these young people were more fortunate than most, because they were here, now, seeing nature and being given the chance to learn about a culture dating back thousands of years, one that was

135

based on the very essence of life itself. Although it was only for a short time, this was better than nothing and thanks to this they were being given the opportunity to do something for nature and for humanity.

The youngsters also learned that in recent years the number of people coming to the highland pastures had dwindled. For this reason, most of the yayla huts were not being used anymore. This was yet another sign of the gradual disappearance of a productive and natural culture, one that had been sustained over millennia, and its loss was truly regrettable. Hearing this, Sinem couldn't hold back her feelings a moment longer: "Isn't there any way to revive this culture?"

It was Ay who answered this question; her pride showing in her voice: "We started the Sun Village project in order to save a vital culture for humanity and pass it from generation to generation. I just hope we're successful."

Until now, the German professor had been sitting listening attentively. He was extremely impressed by what he'd heard, and now wished to say a few words himself: "I've been carrying out research on Anatolian village culture for a few years now and I'm deeply saddened to see that this incredibly rich culture is in danger of disappearing. But now, albeit a bit late, I see that you're now actively involved in doing something to preserve this culture. This is a remarkable development and I would like to congratulate you."

Taking a deep breath, the professor continued: If you've no objection," he said, "I'd like to take part in these activities. I will speak with the German authorities and see if they can grant some funding for this project. What's more, perhaps I could come here with my students and we could join in your efforts, if you'd like us to." As the project leader, it was Güneş who thanked the professor: "Well, I think your offer's

136

totally amazing," he said. "This culture isn't only ours, it's part of humanity's common heritage. We'd be very happy to accept your generous contribution and you're welcome to join us." This was pretty good progress.

The rest of the day was also momentous. The students walked through the mountains, making a study of the plants and flowers with the biologist who'd accompanied them. They learnt the names of several species of plant that were endemic; in other words, specific to this locality. And of course, they took hundreds of photographs.

By the time they got home to their lodgings, everyone was feeling totally exhausted, but nobody complained. This was because it was the first time, they had ever been so close to nature and with so many new horizons opened to them their awareness and knowledge had increased remarkably.

This expedition had been a new phase in the story of their increasing maturity.

Chapter 6

The Culture House

A Journey to The Past

A group had gathered in a small square and were gazing in admiration at a large arch towering before them. Built from enormous chunks of cut stone, they were debating about whether to walk underneath it, as they were concerned that the arch could collapse. This was because the stones looked extremely heavy; each one must have weighed several tons. The arch had been there since ancient times and, looking at it, it was clear that there was nothing holding these stones together.

Güneş walked through the arch. Standing underneath it, he announced, "Come on friends!" First the teachers and then the students began to pass through the archway. It was fine! In the end, no one felt afraid at all...

Having passed through the arch the place where they found themselves was much larger than they thought possible, and the sky above them stretched to the horizon. Trembling, they feel as if they'd somehow arrived on top of the world. In fact, they were standing on the rocky summit of a mountain with deep gullies below them. Then their gaze shifted towards a row of huge statues along the side of the square. Each one was a figure of a person. The young friends examined them carefully, trying to work out who they were. There was a total of five effigies; two on each side and one right in the middle of the arch.

One of the youngsters, Sibel, cried out, "I know this one! It's a statue of the Mother Goddess, Cybele." Everybody began looking more closely at this statue and someone enquired:

"How do you know?" Although everyone had heard of the Goddess Cybele, how could she be so certain that this one was her? Excited, Sibel continued: "We went to Çorum on a school trip once and visited Boğazköy. There, we saw the statues of the gods in Hattusa, the Hittite capital. There was a big statue of Cybele there and this one looks exactly the same." Another friend came forward: "Yes, yes." he said. "She's just liked the Cybele statue I've seen in my history books." Güneş and the rest of the Children of the Sun were delighted by this realization. Someone had been able to recognise this statue as the goddess that symbolized Anatolian Culture. Turning to his friend Doğa, Güneş said: "Look! There are still people who remember you!"

For a moment everyone was silent, and then they all started to laugh. Doğa then began to explain: "This statue belongs to Cybele, the Goddess of Nature. As we all know, Cybele has been the mother goddess of the Anatolian people for as long as eight thousand years. The Mother Goddess represents nature and she also created the world's first value-system. The teachings of the Mother Goddess passed from generation to generation and from land to land. It was Cybele who led to the birth of many civilisations.

The Hittites called her Kubaba, the Phrygians, Cybele. She was Artemis to the Ancient civilizations of the Aegean. There is a famous statue of Kubaba in Çorum's Boğazköy and another of Artemis, which you can see in the Ephesus Museum. The Temple of Artemis, one of the seven wonders of the ancient world, is in Ephesus. Cybele was born in Anatolia, but her fame spread throughout the world. Centuries later, her teachings came to Europe, where she became known as Sibyl, Sibel or Sybele.

How could this belief exist for eight or nine thousand years and then suddenly disappear? How could these teachings

139

have become a mere footnote in history? The best thing to do was to ask an archaeologist; someone, who could tell them how such a thing could have happened. They all turned towards a young man, looking at him with inquisitive eyes… Anlı Bey, was indeed an archaeologist, and a very good one, who had dreamed about being an archaeologist since he was a child. He had read a vast number of books and carried out prodigious amounts of research.

What's more, he was an extremely fortunate archaeologist, principally because he had been born in a country that has some of the most famous ancient sites that have ever existed. Even so, it wouldn't be easy for him to answer the students' questions; in fact, it would be really hard.

Therefore, even Anlı Bey had to think for a moment or two before he could reply: "Well, as you know," he began, "Thousands of years ago, there was no such thing as writing. But people had to find some way of passing on their experiences to future generations. And it was due to this that the oral tradition began. First of all, these types of oral narrative began with honorifics, such as poems, tales, stories and folk music. Then it was followed by sculptures, different types of illustrative symbols, annual feasts and rites. Every story was added to these chronicles. And it was in this way that the Mother Goddess Cybele also came to be."

Everybody was silent, hanging on Anlı Bey's every word. "The Mother Goddess represents every aspect of life," he continued, "including motherhood, birth, procreation, abundance and vitality; in other words, nature in her entirety. The issues covered by these, combined with the rules for life, were transformed into a belief in the divine, which is symbolised by the Mother Goddess Cybele. In other words, belief in this Anatolian goddess was like a kind of 'central ed-

140

ucation system', which amassed information about how people could live. It's also the main reason why we've survived until today. Aren't we still using this vital knowledge, which came about as a result of our ancestors' life experiences?"

Anlı Bey was able to understand from the expressions on his listeners' faces that they had clearly understood what he had told them. But Doğa felt the need to say something too: "Yes," she said. "We're still using the teachings we learned from our ancestors; yes, even today. But, there's an important difference: Cybele is gone; she's no more. Instead, Gods and beliefs that aren't related to the realities of life have taken her place. The Mother Goddess, who taught us to believe that nature is divine, no longer exists. Nature is no longer believed to be sacred. It has now become an exploitable, consumable, destructible commodity. People who destroy nature are the ones who are chiefly responsible for the current natural disasters, destruction and global climate change. It's not possible to live without nature nowadays, any more than it was in the past, and we need to understand that we must have faith in and respect Nature more than ever."

The listeners were nodding in agreement. They all got her message perfectly.

Then, out of nowhere, one of the students whose name was Umar, jubilantly exclaimed: "Hey, I recognize this statue!" Everyone stared at her. Normally known as the shyest girl in the group, she was pointing excitedly at the massive statue in front of her. When she saw that she had everyone's attention, she bowed, before saying: "I'd like to introduce you to the Sky God, Tarhu!" They all looked at the figure carefully. It was said that this God had made heaven and earth tremble. Gök wanted to be the one who explained about the Sky God, whose name he bore.

141

"The Sky God has an important place in Anatolian culture. His name can be seen in many civilizations. In the Hittite civilization it's Hattusa, while the Hurrian people used to call him Taru, Teşup or Tarhu. He was called Istar by the Sumerians. In Ancient Greece he was called Zeus. The Turks thought it fitting to call him Gök Tanrı – Sky God. People used to stare at the heavens – the sky and the stars. They were aware that there was a great universe out there.

They also realised that everything that came from the sky somehow affected them. The God of the Sky was also the God of Abundance; he made the seasons and thanks to him the crops grew. However, when he became angry, he used to roar like thunder and bring lightning and rain. He could also cause drought, so it wasn't a good idea to do anything bad or that annoyed him. The rain prayer we say today must be a tradition originating from the teachings of the Sky God."

Feeling nervous, Umar took a breath. Now it was her turn to speak: "I studied the Sky Gods at school. There are societies that believe in Sky Gods all over the world and we need to be clear about something: having faith in a Sky God is not nonsense. Neither is it an empty metaphysical belief. It is directly related to the realities of life. It's partly due to this that climatology and climate culture have developed. Agriculture also developed and has survived until today, due to this culture. In the days before writing, knowledge about the sky amassed in the oral literature. This in turn created today's climate and astronomy sciences."

These last words really got the young people thinking. It could only mean one thing: their ancestors investigated the natural events that affected them, or that they were able to see directly with their own eyes. That is to say, they investigated and understood what they experienced according to the outlook at that particular time. All things considered; their ancestors had reached a realistic approach earlier than them.

They examined the sky, the seasons; in short, they examined nature. After collecting useful information, they represented them in stories, tales, poems and folk songs via oral literature. Therefore, they passed their information to new generations. Sky God belief was not a metaphysical belief, it was a cultural background of information related to the sky.

This time, another group was gathered in front of the largest statue and they were trying to work out who it could be. Who could this extraordinarily beautiful woman, whose hair appeared to sprout from her head like flames, represent? It was Güneş who recognised her, so he provided the answer. "This statue represents the God of Gods, Arinna. Arinna was the Goddess of the Sun. In Anatolian culture, she was acknowledged as the chief god, the God of Gods. Almost all Anatolian peoples used to believe in Arinna. She was the Chief God of the indigenous peoples of Anatolia; the Hattians and the Hittites."

Hearing this explanation made the other recall her too. Yes! Of course, they had heard of this famous goddess, Arinna, and had read about her in history books, seen her in museums. Some had seen the huge relief of this goddess on a wall, while on a trip to the sacred city of Alacahöyük. So, this was a statue of the famous Sun Goddess, who had been worshipped by their predecessors.

The god of the Hattians, the Goddess Arinna, later became the chief goddess of the Hittites. The Hittites built great cities and temples in the name of this god and they used to hold feasts in her honour. Although she had different names over time, Arinna used to be worshipped across Anatolia, long before the arrival of Christianity and Islam.

Arinna is known to have been a belief system. However, she represented much more important values too. She represented one of humanity's most important cultures, one that contributed to and guided the development of humankind. Many Anatolian civilisations flourished and offered insights into the world, thanks to Arinna.

Güneş was about to continue but one student couldn't resist asking: "The worship of Arinna lasted for such a long time. What do you think the secret of this is? This was a question a young history teacher had been looking forward to hearing. Taking a deep breath, he slowly began to explain, in a voice that sounded as if it came from the deep, reaching out across the ages. "Not only was Arinna a belief system, she represented a Sun Culture that existed for thousands of years. As you know, the sun is the source of all life.

The sun is responsible for everything that happens in the world. Sunshine is the energy that warms the planet, creates the seasons, and keeps all living things alive. People who have observed this simple and scientific truth believed in this and held their beliefs for eons. As the source of this belief, the sun was also adopted as a symbol. That's why this statue was erected."

These were impressive words. They now understood the reason why their ancestors had attached so much importance to the sun...

On the right, next to the Sky God, was another statue. The group was curious about who this beautiful female could be. Maybe they were gazing at a statue of the most beautiful woman in the world. Her appearance was totally captivating. Suddenly, Ay stepped forward and asked her stunned companions: "How could you not recognize me?"

Ay was undeniably the loveliest girl in the village. She was certainly as beautiful as the female statue. Her gaze roamed over the effigy in complete fascination, before focusing on the eyes. Her words were so close to the truth that nobody felt the need to laugh. No words were necessary. This statue that Ay was standing next to was totally lifelike.

"As you understand," she continued, "I represent the moon in the sky, which makes you feel boundless emotions. I sometimes appear in your dreams. I play with people's hearts and give them beautiful, sensual feelings. I am the symbol of love and romance. I am the Goddess of Love." Ay's sweet words brought smiles to everyone's faces. But they were looking as if they wanted to hear more... "People made me a symbol of their love and erected my statue," she continued. "They wrote poems and sang folk songs about me and I didn't hang around; I tried to add colour to their nights."

There was no need to say any more. These words reminded them of beautiful Aphrodite, Eros, and many stories and legends. Everyone was suffused with an inner glow, which filled their minds and bodies. The feelings that accompanied these lovely words also meant that some of them couldn't help but catch each other's eye!

It was time to learn about the last statue. Güneş couldn't wait a moment longer and gave the stage to Su: "This statue is the Goddess of Water," began Su. "This god is one of the most loved gods in our part of the world. Water has always been sacred to the people of Anatolia. And there are many sayings that are believed to have originated from this belief, such as 'Su gibi aziz ol', which are still often used here in Anatolia today. Water was considered to be the source of life on earth and it has always been revered. All sentient beings value water because they know that it's impossible to live without it."

By now it was evening and as night fell, they headed back. But, before the young people left, they couldn't resist looking at the statues one last time. This short trip had deeply impressed them and had given new meaning to their lives. It hadn't been easy, but in a remarkably short space of time they'd experienced ten thousand years of Anatolian culture and learned lots of new and worthwhile things. They'd also seen how it still influences them today.

Anatolia – what a wonderful place – and with such an amazing culture!

A Great Day

A large crowd had gathered on a road below the village. Everyone was talking eagerly with each other. It was rumoured that there was something unusual happening in the village. But what? Two people who were visiting the village approached the gathering. What they saw was an ordinary ground-breaking ceremony. But when they looked more carefully, they noticed a man in a suit and tie, evidently from the city, cutting a red ribbon. The governor was also there, sitting in the front row. So, this was obviously not an ordinary event at all.

They eavesdropped on what the governor was saying: "Today," he announced, "we are going to start constructing the most important building in this community, the Village Culture House. Thanks to these houses, thousands of years of village culture will be safeguarded and improved. In the process, this culture will spread, first throughout the country and eventually the world. Until now, the significance of village culture has remained unknown but, developments in the last decade have made us aware of how important they are. As a consequence, eco-tourism has become increasingly appealing. One of the aims of this culture house is to enable the development of tourism. This will be the first culture centre of many. Good luck to everyone involved!"

The villagers attending the ceremony looked very happy. It was the first time someone had paid any attention to their culture and a centre was being built to protect it and revive it. They were grateful to the people that got the ball rolling so that this could happen. Everybody turned to the project's architects, the Children of the Sun. It was necessary to say something, wasn't it? As had become the custom, it was Güneş who spoke: "While we were visiting your houses and asking everyone about their hopes and expectations, we came

147

across some very important issues. We saw many precious items in each house that couldn't be bought today. Each one of them could impress the world of high style and fashion, such as clothing, colourful carpets, kilims, ornaments, lace, embroideries and the like. They were all beautiful and authentic. It was all well worth seeing, especially all the stuff our grannies had tucked away in their dowry chests. But what bothered us, is that these hidden treasures are mouldering away and will eventually disappear.

"To begin with, we couldn't work out how to make the most of these wonderful things. Having thought long and hard, we've finally come to the decision that they should go on display, so that artists and art lovers can come and see them. We shared this idea with our villagers, and everyone has been very enthusiastic about the plan. One person went so far as to suggest that we could develop the idea further and start producing more of these things, which could be even more beautiful! The interest has been really encouraging, so we began to discuss the idea with everyone in the village, and this new model for a Culture Centre is the result!"

"Why is it being called a *new model*?" someone in the crowd enquired. "What's the difference between this and the old one?" Güneş answered without any hesitation: "Actually, our first thought was to use an existing model. But we changed our minds when we looked at these, as some cultural centres were sometimes closed, locked up, as if they were a business. They weren't opened unless important visitors came along, and some weren't fit for purpose. What's more they brought the villages unnecessary expense. Also, there wasn't any suitable place in the building to produce anything."

The Governor listened with interest to this exchange. It was true, the state had not properly maintained culture houses and traditional village properties in these settlements. Almost none of them were working. These young people said they were developing a new model and they wanted help. He could transfer some money from the village protection fund to the village development fund. He was curious about the model that the young people would develop.

Meanwhile, Güneş continued: "Many reasons have been influential in the development of the culture house. First of all, the culture house must not be for show. These must be places of which villagers want to take ownership, embrace, use, live in and look after. But there is another, much more important thing… and this is that manufacturing in the village has pretty much ground to a halt. To regenerate it, this cultural centre should be inspiring and contain a feature that will reignite our villager's enthusiasm for making things. In addition to this, traditional architecture in our village has already been ruined, and new, bad and impersonal, so-called 'modern' constructions are being built. This cultural centre must be built using this village's traditional architecture. Also, the building must have its own architectural style, one that benefits from the sun and doesn't use air-polluting fossil fuels."

It was clear to Güneş that everybody was listening carefully, as indeed they were. It was as if he was articulating their own thoughts. Güneş and the other Children of the Sun really were exceptional young people. They had done the research, examined everything in detail and discovered the right solutions for the future. They were able to come up with realistic projects that could respond to the many problems in the village… but were far from being self-centred. Which architect or planner would be able to do this...?

Güneş finished his speech with these words: "We hope that this new cultural centre will contribute to the development and improvement of our village. We also hope it will provide a good example for our neighbourhood and our country." As he finished speaking, the crowd began to applaud. Then Güneş cut the red ribbon together with the Governor. And so, the construction of the Culture House began…

The cultural centre would be built by the students working in cooperation with local crafts, under the supervision of the university staff. Most of the students returned to their hometowns at the end of the first week, while the architecture and planning students began the second stint of their summer internship. It is they who would be doing the construction work.

They all knew that the building they were creating would not be an ordinary structure. It would be used to fulfil very important functions, and they had faith in their ability to work conscientiously and hard.

About the Sun Culture

It was almost evening. The first day's work was over, and the students had gathered with the younger teachers in the garden of a village house. They were deep in conversation.

One of the friends said: "Do you know, I'm so glad I came to this village." Another added: "Me, too. There's something about this place that I find really fascinating. I feel as if I'm in a different world." One of the young teachers joined in: "You are so right. I'd never heard anything positive about villagers and village culture. Quite the opposite, I was told that there were health problems in villages and that villagers were bad, illiterate and ignorant."

Another assistant spoke up: "Before coming here, I thought the same. But since meeting and getting to know the villagers here, my opinion has changed. I now realise how I wrong I was." This prompted another comment: "Do you know, I think we've become strangers to our own culture. We've forgotten how rich our culture is. We've become used to superficial western ways of life, such as hamburgers, cola and fast food. Our love of all things western is destroying us. We've reached the stage where we can't recognise ourselves anymore."

Gök, who had been listening intently to what was being said, now joined the conversation: "Atatürk said, 'the villager is the master of the nation' but nobody believed these words. Atatürk and his associates, who founded our Republic [of Turkey], wanted development to start with the villagers but it didn't happen. Back in 1940, they established Village Institutes for this very purpose; a new education system, which was unparalleled in the rest of the world. But some called them 'communist nests' and closed them down. As a result, these schools, which could have led to the development of

151

Anatolia's rural areas, were brought to an end, even though they were in fact one of the most important strongholds of the Turkish revolution.

The history teacher intervened: "But there were external powers that wanted to hinder the Turkish Revolution and put a stop to it. There're loads of information that proves your words are true. Our history is full of such evidence. But the real question we need to ask ourselves is why we don't have ownership of our own culture? We don't, do we?" These were issues that have been debated and disputed for years. Güneş and his friends didn't want to become involved in what could only become a circular argument. They preferred to come up with fresh ideas.

Ay decided it was time to change the subject: "Did you know that Anatolia has a special and rich sun culture that's still unknown? I think this is the subject we should be discussing. In fact, because of issues such as climate change, and the natural disasters that have been happening in recent years, the sun has finally made it onto the world's agenda. However, long before people began to use oil or nuclear energy, they lived with the sun for millennia and developed modes of production that made the most of the sun. We need this cultural accumulation, even if people don't know it, much, much more than we did in the past."

One of the groups, who didn't know about the subject asked: "What do you mean by solar culture? Su answered this question: "In the past, when there was no oil or nuclear energy or coal, production was made using the sun and natural energy derivatives, such as wind, water or biomass. Doğa stepped in: "You remember the sun civilizations? We can list the many civilizations that existed in the past. There was the Egyptian, the Aztec, the Inca and the Anatolian civilizations. They used the sun not only as energy, but in other areas too, such as solar cities, agriculture, solar architecture and some forms of food production."

Another student spoke up: "But nowadays we can't do anything without oil and coal. We can't plough our fields or plant crops. We can't get warm when the weather's cold and we can't get cool when it's hot. Most important is transport. Modern transport runs on gasoline." He was right. Nowadays, changing all these systems would be impossible. Dreaming like this was futile!

Güneş could sense a negative atmosphere, and immediately went into action: "Of course, you're absolutely right. Without oil we couldn't survive. All kinds of technologies depend on oil. But as long as solar technology continues to develop, solving these problems will eventually become simple. Don't forget, there are already planes and cars being produced that run on solar energy. And, as production systems advance, we'll be able to build towns and cities without the need for oil."

In a single moment, these words changed the atmosphere from negative to positive. Could his words be right? Could the things he was saying be possible? If so, why hadn't anyone begun to do something? But Güneş hadn't finished: "We're all born into a system, and this system – namely capitalism – is the one in which we all find ourselves captive. Nevertheless, as we gain insight, and try to fulfil the requirements of our enlightenment, we can overcome these difficulties; through our own efforts, as well as those of universities, and NGOs, and particularly with the efforts of our young people."

"But…" someone said, "what can *we* do? All these powers are in the hands of multinational companies. If they wanted to, they could destroy us at the drop of a hat." "Come on!

153

Let's not be so pessimistic," retorted Güneş. "The world is changing from day to day. Because of climate change, we must closely monitor any positive improvements in the world, and we need to assess any opportunities that arise immediately." "How so?" asked one of them. "Well, although I'm young too," confessed Güneş, "I sometimes have difficulty understanding today's youngsters. Some set up organizations to change the world, while others come together to stop these changes, such as factories that pollute the environment. None of these are wrong in themselves; they are all genuine opinions, logical actions, but there's something missing."

One of the parties couldn't stop themselves from asking, "Is it our friends who are doing the wrong things?" "Although they believe their opposition to be correct, the results are ineffective," said Güneş. "Despite the revolutionary struggles that have been taking place since the beginning of the last century, socialist countries have disappeared, while capitalism has expanded and spread throughout the world. And have you taken a look at the environment? As environmental awareness has increased, activities have also increased. There have been many innovations and great strides taken to keep the environment clean, but sadly there's been no reduction in environmental pollution. Quite the contrary, it's increased and has begun to threaten life on earth. Something's gone terribly wrong." "What do *you* think's gone wrong?" someone else asked. "Personally, rather than fight against capitalism, I think we must focus on significant projects that can save humanity."

"What you're saying is great, but none of it's possible," added another. "Why not?" challenged Güneş. "We young ones all know what the problems are. If we don't want the environment to be polluted, we can develop technologies or systems that don't pollute it. If we want to stop climate change, we can set up systems using the sun and natural resources, rather than those that cause global warming. In other words, we can establish energy systems based on the sun. We must try to make the right choices, ones that will change the structures that drive the system of exploitation by the energy monopolies. In short; it would be better for us to follow a constructive, creative and productive path, not a quarrelsome one."

The youngsters were astonished; at least, at first. Important things were being said that could totally change their opinions. But even though they thought they were right, it seemed unlikely that what was being suggested would ever be successful. Someone voiced an objection: "Even if the goals you've mentioned are productive, I don't think they'd have much of an impact." "You're right," said someone else.

Once again, Güneş was ready with an answer. "It's not enough just to produce or think about being productive. We'd have to take things a step further. It's not possible to get successful results without the right strategy. Perhaps I could explain it like this: you've probably all heard of something called the butterfly effect. It means that everything in the world affects everything else. The entire future of the world could change just because a butterfly flaps its wings. This is our strategy. It's related to a skill, which is to be able to carry out the correct project at the correct time and in the correct place."

According to some people, Güneş was rather a strange young man, who thought differently, and sometimes spoke without restraint. Or maybe he was just a dreamer? "What you're saying is right, but how could we carry out the correct projects? Could you give us some examples please?" This question was asked by a student, whose name was Yağmur. Yağmur had asked the question that many had wanted to ask.

155

By now it was very late, and so Ay's answer bought the discussions to an end with these words: "The butterfly effect that we believe we can create will be with the world's first architectural example of the solar-powered, culture house project that we started here today, together, in this village."

A Living Wall

The construction of the cultural centre was going well, and the students worked with boundless enthusiasm and commitment. The words with which Ay had concluded the previous night's conversation had deeply affected them and they were now beginning to think that they were there for a much larger purpose. Her words had touched a chord with these youngsters. First, the foundations had been laid and the main walls rose from them. To begin the footings were filled with rubble and then the entire floor was insulated. Thermal pipes were then placed horizontally, followed by a layer of topsoil, and divisions were laid out using stones gathered from a nearby stream.

Those watching the construction couldn't make any sense of what was going on. They just assumed that the young people must have some idea. As always, some tried to interfere, but they were politely ignored, and construction continued apace. Within a week, the outer walls of the building could be seen. They consisted of two parts. There was the main wall built using granite and another behind. It was this that started to attract attention. When the villagers asked Güneş why this was so, he avoided giving them answers.

The central wall was two-storeys high and the connections between the walls were made using beams. The walls were built without mortar and the gap between the two walls were filled with rubble. They had left a larger gap in the middle of the wall. As far as those watching were concerned, it all looked very odd. An architect who came to inspect progress was pleased with these developments; he was also satisfied that the money had been spent correctly. In fact, he also wondered whether they were doing something wrong, as he too thought the wall was strange. At first, he considered intervening, but he changed his mind as the building was obviously special.

"The construction is going very well, I congratulate you," he confirmed. Even so, he couldn't resist saying to Güneş, "But, to be honest, I don't really understand that middle wall. Why are you building it like this? What's its purpose?" So far, Güneş had not told anyone about the wall. He was keeping the whole thing a secret and until now hadn't intended to share it. But, in view of the architect's curiosity, Güneş drew the architect aside and in a low voice explained its purpose to him.

It was very clear that he didn't want anybody else to hear what he was saying: "We were planning on keeping this information for the opening ceremony," he whispered under his breath, "but I'll tell you now if you like. This is an example of a special kind of wall, one that for hundreds of years our ancestors used to build. One of our postgrad students has called it a "living wall". It's one that used to be regularly used in settlements on the Taurus Mountains and we're building it to the authentic design. Its distinctive feature is that it has high thermostatic properties."

Even though the architect was relatively experienced he had no idea what Güneş was talking about. "Okay, that's fine… Please do as you wish," he said, trying to look as if he understood. Later, they would learn that the architect had given a positive report to the governor about the construction, but he didn't say anything about the living wall. As the height of the building increased, other things also attracted attention. The massive outer walls, ninety centimetres in width, continued to the upper floors.

Part of the roof was closed, while another part was left open. The ground floor was divided into two areas, and the floor above included two rooms and another area of about two-hundred square meters was left bare. This was another mystery. By now, a third of the building had been completed. It was still only two storeys high, but the height of the walls had been increased by about one meter. This led to more speculation with some of the villagers asking each other if such a building was even possible.

Time passed and the reason for the mystery finally became clear. During the last week of construction, steel profiles and glass started to arrive. First of all, the various sections were made up and then the triangular frame and eventually the windows were fitted. The solar panels and collectors were placed on top. When the construction was complete, a dome-shaped building appeared in all its glory. However, there was still something strange about it. Half of the building was closed and whiter than white, while the other half of it was transparent. It was certainly very strange and was attracting a lot attention. Whatever could be going on?

Events finally came to a head. There had been as many rumours as there are leaves on a tree, and there was even a leak to the media. But, since the first day, Güneş and his friends had kept their promises to each other and never revealed their secret. They just continued to say, "You'll learn when the time comes."

People from neighbouring villages continued to come and look at the building. They couldn't figure it out either. Along with everyone else, their curiosity would only be satisfied at the opening ceremony.

159

The Culture House

It was the day of the official opening and everybody in the village was rushing around. A great many guests, including special ones like the Governor, were going to come. The ceremony had to do the village justice. Preparations had continued for an entire week, but finally the special day arrived.

A massive crowd had assembled in front of the new building. Inquisitive folk, who'd heard about the new culture house, flooded into the village. As well as the local press, the national press was out in force. Everyone was impatiently waiting for the opening. As is customary, the Governor had the first word. Before making his speech, he contemplated the building. The semi-spherical dome was gleaming; aesthetically, it was stunning.

If truth be told, it suited the village very well. The Governor, who was as curious as anyone to learn the secrets of the building, kept his speech very brief. Basically, he thanked everybody who'd contributed, from the eldest to the youngest, and said he sincerely hoped that the building would reap benefits for the village.

Then it was time for Güneş to speak. After so much research, they had created a very different building, one that nobody had expected. So where would his speech begin? He found the first words really difficult, and had problems getting them out of his mouth, but finally he composed himself and his words began to flow more easily: "I know...," he said, "I'm very aware that we have created an extraordinary building. And we want to explain why we've done this. But, first, we'd like to thank everyone who's supported us; professors, teachers and students, everyone who's worked with us throughout. Thank you all, so much, for everything."

When the applause died down, he continued: "We've thought about this a lot and we're aware that it's going to take a long time to solve all the village's problems individually. It may take a lot of money too and now and again it could be a waste of time. Instead, we've focused on finding strategic solutions which could deliver the progress we seek. The building you see now is the way in which such an idea comes into being. We didn't start off thinking about this model, it emerged spontaneously. Originally, for our first solution, we wanted to find one that was appropriate. We therefore spoke individually with our local people to identify their expectations. From this it became clear that the village had three basic requirements."

What were these three basic requirements of the village? Everyone was totally absorbed by what Güneş was saying. He explained: "The first requirement is related to agricultural production. Everything produced in the village was delayed because of the cold weather and was late reaching the market. Meanwhile, the prices had fallen because the markets were already full to bursting with produce. As a result, our producers could not compete with crops grown in warmer regions. Our villagers asked us for a solution. So, we considered all this carefully and decided that solar energy could help us solve this problem. We focused our work on a "greenhouse model" to accelerate production and extend the growing period, and one that was suitable for cold weather conditions."

By now, everybody was holding their breath. "Here," Güneş said, turning to look at the building, "What you see here, is a highly efficient, high yield solar greenhouse." Everyone, especially the Governor, was listening with rapt attention. Until now, no institution or individual searching for an answer to this problem had come up with a solution like this. It only took a moment for what Güneş had said to sink in before the entire audience rose to their feet again, clapping and shouting "bravo!" The young companions had to wait for the excitement to subside before starting to explain the village's second important expectation.

This time it was Doğa who spoke: "Every crop we grow in the village has ecological features that are sought after in the world. Hormone-free vegetables are produced without toxic chemicals; fruit and plants that grow wild in the forest, winter-foods and dairy products, all of which are natural, organic and delicious. But the villagers can't sell or market them. For this reason, we needed to find solutions for packing and marketing. So, as you can see, there is a food production workshop in this new house."

The villagers were happy to hear this good news. They were finally going to get the food production workshop they had long been waiting for. They applauded with heartfelt emotion. When the applause died down, it was Ay's turn to speak: "The village's artists and young people need an art workshop. While we were visiting the families, we came across many precious works of art and embroideries. We saw colourful examples of original embroideries and lace, knitting and clothes in their grandmas' dowry chests. We saw hand woven decorative carpets and kilims.

"In one house we saw young women making traditional patchwork. Each of these, all of which have artistic value, are like the original examples of patchwork that are now becoming so well-known and sought after today. We need a workshop to develop, recreate and reintroduce these skills and put them back on the map. Therefore, today, we are also opening the Village Art Workshop at our cultural centre." The young women jumped to their feet and clapped for all they were worth until their hands were sore. Their dream had finally come true!

162

It was clear from the look on the Governor's face that he was happy too. He had been to the openings of other villages' cultural centres in the past but none of them had been so fascinating. Now he was witnessing the heartfelt joy of the villagers. These Children of the Sun were really different from any other people he'd ever met. They had managed to achieve something that the state had not. They had brought a project to life that epitomised the village's hopes and dreams.

Even so, the environmentalists who had travelled from far and wide for the opening appeared to be unsatisfied. Yes, the villagers looked very happy, but the environmentalists' concerns were different. They also wanted to see innovations in their fields. It was Gök who realized this, and he immediately responded: "This building has been designed in such a way that we will never need to use coal and oil or other energies that pollute the environment. As you're already aware, the use of energies such as coal, lignite, oil and natural gas, all of which contribute to global warming, is becoming widespread and polluting the villages.

"We needed solutions that both prevent environmental pollution and reduce the use of excessive amounts of wood, which is destroying our forests. As a result, we've developed a new model that considers the Anatolian culture of solar architecture, which we've called the *high efficiency solar house model*. Here, we've preferred to use traditional heating systems. We've endeavoured to build a simple and economical solar house, just as we did with the village house."

One of the environmentalists was curious to learn a little more about this subject: "So, are you saying that you've taken advantage of various aspects of traditional Anatolian architecture? Another asked: "What kind of traditional systems have you used? And does this rather strange wall you've built in the middle have any unusual features? Also, why have you laid underground pipes?

As the number of people asking questions increased, Güneş returned to the discussion, as it was, he who had made the heating and cooling calculations: "Yes," he said. "We've very much benefitted from traditional solar architecture. These systems, the ones that we saw in the Country of the Sun, are those that developed in our country as a result of thousands of years of experience. In this way, we will achieve much greater efficiency than we would with systems being used in today's contemporary architecture."

Güneş was genuinely excited. The time had finally come for him to reveal the secret that people had been curious to hear about for weeks. But he had to be careful, he shouldn't give too much away: "First, I'd like to explain the wall in the middle of the building. You may have heard about walls that benefit from the sun and underground heating, in many areas, including this village. We've examined examples of these walls and have compared efficiency. We've established that the most effective system is the wall used in high areas of the Taurus Mountains."

"What wall do you mean?" asked one of the spectators, a question that Güneş was able to answer immediately. "It's one we've called a *living wall*. Interestingly, it can balance internal and external energies, allowing houses to benefit more from the sun. With these buildings we've taken these systems in hand and tried to make them even more effective." It was the first time the listeners had heard of a living wall or been faced with such a fascinating proposition. "Well?" said someone else, "What do these underground rooms and pipe systems mean?"

Once again, it was Güneş who explained: "First, we were particularly interested to learn how *caravanserais* and *hamams* used to be heated. The Turkish bath, as you know, is world famous. Heating systems are very important for these baths, because of the high temperatures they require. In fact, the system they used was simple but extremely effective." A member of the audience enquired, "Do you mean to say you've used a heating system like those in a Turkish bath?" "Yes," said Güneş. "In a way you could say that. We decided to try a similar system to those used in Turkish baths. But our design is a bit different. We're obtaining solar energy via the greenhouse and are transferring this to an underground heating system. In this way, we've succeeded in getting a more efficient level of heating."

A journalist then asked: "What level of productivity will be achieved for this cold climate? Presumably this has been accounted for?" "Yes, it has," replied Güneş. "In this village the heating period is quite long; we need to keep warm for about eight months. According to our calculations, this building will be able to remain warm for about nine months without needing any other energy resources. As a result, eighty percent of the annual heating requirements will be provided by the sun."

What Güneş was saying was fascinating but hard to believe. In the coldest remaining three months of the year, half of the additional heating requirement would be obtained from the sun's energy and the other half from a vent in the living wall.[7] "So why is the wall two storeys high and built without using

---

[7] *An effective heating system used in Turkish baths, researched by several universities and with some very interesting results. A method called the "smoke heating system" was used in the baths. The walls and enclosed underground areas were heated with the warm smoke of the burning via numerous chimneys. This system has been successfully used in Turkish baths for hundreds of years.*

mortar?" Güneş also tried to explain this question but without going into too much detail: "The solar wall is a new concept that we have specifically developed to make more use of the sun. This wall was built with a thermal layer inside it, to create air currents that would heat more rapidly with the sun and help warm the rear areas of the building."

Although the audience were all ears, many had to admit that they didn't really understand a word of what Güneş was saying but in actual fact, the system was very clear. Just as in Günsera [8], the wall obtains maximum energy from the sun, and the resulting hot air is combined and stored beneath the ground, as heat. The heated air is distributed by the solar wall system in the middle, throughout the entire building. The collector and panel mounted on top of the glass dome also provide the building's hot water and electricity.

One aspect of the building that hadn't so far been discussed was the style in which the building had been constructed. Why was the shape of the culture house so different? It didn't appear to be in keeping with the village's traditional architecture. One of the journalists present expressed such an opinion: "I'm curious to know why you chose the semi-circular shape for the dome. Is there any reason for it?"

"Of course, there's a reason for choosing this shape" said Gök. "The reason why we chose it is mostly related to heating issues. We looked at quite a few examples. This hemisphere has more advantages than either a triangle, a quadrangle or even a pentagonal shape. This shape has a smaller surface layer, so there's not so much heat loss. Perhaps this is

---

[8] *Günsera is the first solar-powered greenhouse in Turkey. It is cooperation of search and development by METU and Ankara University and it has been developed for Güneşköy greenhouse research. It is open for visits. (Look for the book Günsera, Ankara, 1912 and the film of Günsera on YouTube)*

the same reason why our ancestors preferred using domes in larger buildings such as mosques, hammams and caravanserais. And, this together with it being one of the most significant features of Anatolian architecture, is why we decided to use it."

After Gök's speech the applause continued for ages. But finally, the time came for cutting the ribbon. Ay and the Governor cut it together and then everybody began to explore the building and the systems they had just heard about.

The culture centre also had a very beautiful garden. The landscape architects and the biology students had worked together to create a magnificent outdoor space, using only local plants and flowers. The garden also made the most of solar energy.

Everyone who'd come to see the new building was smiling.

Chapter 7

Eco-tourism

Kermes - The Sun Festival

Güneş and his friends had got together and were going over the developments. In a short time, they had managed to achieve many great things, but they didn't consider these to be enough. It was time to start working on new projects for the village.

Güneş was first to speak: "I think the things we've done so far have to a certain extent helped to revive the village and increase production and efficiency. But we shouldn't limit ourselves to these. We have to develop new projects. "What kind of projects?" asked Gök. But before Güneş could reply, Ay intervened: "In my mind, we should promote the village's art and handicrafts. I think that'd be a good place to start." Güneş agreed. To be sure, there were some interesting arte-facts hidden away in the village and they should be exhibited in some way.

But Su had a different idea. "The village has so many deli-cious and natural food products," she said, "and what's more, they're organic too. As far as I'm concerned, we need to find markets to sell them, which will also help the village's econ-omy." And Doğa suggested yet a different plan: "Shouldn't we start by introducing the natural beauty and culture of the village?"

Everyone was right... They were all great suggestions but all the same, no one knew where to begin. After a lengthy dis-cussion they decided to promote the village products and hold an exhibition of them, in which everybody could partic-

ipate. They shared their idea with the local people and received lots of positive feedback. Now they needed to promote it.

It was the first time that university students had come to village and shared the routine of daily life with the local people.
This had made everyone very happy but now, sadly, they had
gone. The university teachers and students had returned to
their urban lives – leaving the villagers alone again.

Everyone felt very sad, especially the elderly villagers, who
had become used to having the young people around, and
now looked upon them as members of their own family. They
had meant much more to them than ordinary guests would
have. The students and the families with whom they'd stayed
had met up in the square on departure day. There had been a
prevailing feeling of sadness and heartfelt emotion; so much
so, that some people had even shed some tears.

Most of the villagers liked the young people's idea of promoting the village but even so, there were a few who didn't.
"Who needs them?" they'd say. "Those foreigners, they'll
come to our village and do nothing but ruin our peace and
quiet!" But these opinions were fairly few and far between.
When it was clear that the vast majority of the village people
supported it, a meeting was organised, at which the Muhtar
came up with a different idea: "It'll soon be time for our traditional harvest festival. Couldn't we include the promotion
with these festivities?" he suggested.

"…And do them both together. Of course! That's a brilliant
idea," said Güneş. "Would it be ok with you if the Children
of the Sun took responsibility for organising this year's festival?" The village committee was delighted by this offer; the
young people would be taking on a significant responsibility.
Everyone immediately agreed without hesitation. Güneş and

his friends were pleased too. They would be undertaking two worthwhile jobs both at the same time, making both the festival and the promotion much more successful. However, this year's developments in the village were different, so the festival also had to be different... But how?

They thought long and hard. The solar projects had aroused great interest, which festivals and promotional events should help to increase interest in this and similar projects throughout the country. Finally, they decided it would be better to organize a culture-specific Kermes, an event that would combine both the sun culture and the harvest festival.

They prepared a schedule and then started work. News of the Kermes was met with great excitement throughout the village. When the villagers heard about the programme, which wasn't going to be just about entertainment but also to promote the village's culture and produce, they liked it too. [9]

There was now a great commotion as both the village and its products had to be well promoted. Everyone started rushing around in preparation. Güneş and his friends visited each house to choose the artefacts that would be exhibited. All of these were carried to the culture centre, where they attached the written labels.

---

[9] *A similar festival was held in Ürünlü village, Antalya, which attracted great interest. Much has been said and written about this project, which had big repercussions in Turkey; there were, however, some problems during the implementation phase. The funds were withdrawn as they were not used appropriately by the politicians and authorities. In contrast we achieved our purpose as the villagers were able to apply this project by themselves. The houses have been put under protection; some houses were used as pensions. The infrastructure was renewed; streets were furnished using stones instead of concrete. Village handicraft workshops were opened, as well as food restaurants and markets selling local produce (for more information look at the internet website: Ürünlü Culture Village Project or Ürünlü Cultural Village Project report, by the Ministry of Culture and Tourism and Governor of Antalya. (Ç.G. Antalya 2010, with Picture on page 216.)*

The Muhtar and committee were particularly interested in this promotion, as it would be the first time such an event had been held in the village and the village produce would be on display for the first time too. The success of this exhibition could affect the village's future, and this was one of the main reasons for everyone's excitement.

In line with the programme, the entire village was declared an exhibition space. First of all, the Fire Square was decorated with traditional agricultural tools. Old pots and pans and copper and steel items were stacked neatly in the square. In another square, under the leadership of Sis Hanım, traditional patchwork rugs, carpets and costumes made by the village women, and weaving looms, would be exhibited. Charming examples of ceramics, some which the villagers had made themselves and kept from the year dot, were chosen and placed in a corner. Labels were attached on each piece on which was written when and by whom they had been made.

While these preparations were going on, Ay and Güneş were making banners and posters, which they decorated with sun symbols. They also made invitations and these they sent to the relevant people. The main accommodation was already prepared but in addition to these, there were also areas designated for parking, camping and caravans.

The opening day finally came. The villagers were waiting anxiously. They wondered if people would come or would all their work be in vain? Such was the apprehension, some of the villagers hardly slept the night before. Some even had strange dreams. But, as they all knew, nothing could be done at this stage and they would all have to wait patiently.

Those who came along very early were crestfallen, as nothing was going on. It was about nine o'clock when the first visitors began to arrive and there were enough to make the villagers hopeful. But, after ten o'clock the multitudes descended and by noon, the village was almost too crowded.

The villagers' faces were all broad smiles; they were very happy indeed. Now, there was another flurry of activity: how could the villagers feed so many people and where would they stay?

The guests were visiting the exhibitions, asking for information from guides and taking photographs. The hungry and the thirsty could either buy something from the exhibited products or shop at the food stalls and buffets that had been set up in the village squares.

By now, every corner of the village was crowded with visitors and all the stalls in the squares had long queues. There was everything, from farming produce to handmade artistic creations and every stall attracted attention. But undoubtedly the most popular area was the one where there were stalls selling organic, dried or bottled fruit and vegetables. There was one section selling numerous varieties of medicinal herbs, plants, mushrooms, cornelian cherries and wild strawberries, all collected from the yayla and the forests. Here too there were massive crowds in front of every stall.

Almost every young person in the village was taking part in the organization. Some of them were responsible for welcoming the visitors. Others were working as guides, showing people around the town. The rest of them were doing the tasks Güneş and his friends gave them. They were all dressed in their traditional costumes and all the while, there was the light and beautiful sound of folk music being played: songs, dances and melodies from this part of Turkey.

The visitors were astonished by the atmosphere in the village. With its traditional houses, Turkish folk music, streets and squares it was as if a mysterious world had emerged from the pages of a colourful history book. Everybody was wandering around the village, full of curiosity and excitement, watching, contemplating, asking questions and learning. The village house which was restored according to its original design and used as a coffee shop and guest house, was one of the places most visited. During the festival it also served as a traditional *aşevi*.

The visitors couldn't hide their admiration for the beauty of the newly restored village houses. The culture house, on the other hand, provided a completely different focus of interest. Ay was responsible for introducing the centre and entertaining the guests. She provided information about the sun project and architecture and solar culture. She also made a tour of an amazing place called the 'original products garden,' which had become a source of pride for the whole village.

In truth, the visitors experienced a day that was filled with traditional culture. The group overheard visitors saying that they had never before seen or heard of such an interesting place and they also heard them discussing sun culture in Anatolian villages, something that made Güneş and his friends particularly joyful. This was because Anatolian Sun Culture, the subject of all their hard work, had finally become a major topic for discussion.

By now it was evening and beginning to get dark. Everyone was thinking what a great day they'd had, even better than they'd expected, when suddenly, the lights went off. Everywhere was plunged into darkness. What was happening? At the same moment, flames began to rise from the middle of the village. Everybody was astounded, rather curious and a little bit scared.

There appeared to be a massive blaze rising from the middle of the village. The flames were so huge that they lit up the sky. In fact, the young people of the village had revived the eternal flame in the village square, and the flames were a kind of summons to attend. And that's exactly what happened. When people saw the flames, they started heading towards them.

Now the festivities could begin!

The Feast

The square was overflowing with people. Flames lit up the night sky. The Muhtar was already standing on the platform ready to give his speech. He was watching the crowd, waiting for everyone to settle down. Finally, as he said, "Dear guests," a hush fell.

"On behalf of our village, I would like to thank every one of you so very much for coming and visiting our festival today. Truly, *Sağolun, var olun*; thank you, may you live long. As you can see, we've made a change to this year's traditional *şenlik*. We've also provided an opportunity for our villagers to exhibit all kinds of products, produced by them, throughout the course of the festival. As you can see this has met with great interest. A variety of foods and drinks, preserves and cheeses, all specific to our village, are attracting the attention of manufacturers, as well as visitors coming here for the first time.

"Some companies will form partnerships with our villagers with a view to making joint productions. From all this it would appear that we will have to work even harder and produce more. This we understand. Even products that are not so important to us appear to be of great interest, something that will provide us and villages everywhere with new business opportunities that will stimulate our country's economy. For this reason, I would like to say that we are more than happy with what's happening. So, on behalf of the village, I would like to express our sincerest thanks to Güneş and his friends, who started these developments and have worked persistently to evaluate the opportunities and make them happen, and everyone else who has supported them."

The Muhtar's speech certainly hit the right note; everybody was standing, and the applause continued for minutes on end.

Actually, the young people had overcome the deteriorating condition of the village and also revived the bad economy. To those involved, these things felt like miracles. The young friends genuinely deserved much more than applause.

After the Muhtar, Güneş stepped onto the platform. He gazed at the scene before him. This, the largest open space in the village, the balconies, the gardens, everywhere was overflowing with people. This was a sign that clearly showed him how incredibly successful they'd been. But Güneş was a modest young man and didn't want to brag. For him, a dignified speech was essential.

"As a matter of fact," he said, "we haven't really done that much. All we wanted to do was to look after and protect our ancestors' culture. To be honest, we would never have guessed that all this work could be taken on and completed in such a short time. I am just wondering whether we could describe this development as a cultural explosion. So often the shops and markets are full of worthless, characterless, impersonal, identical goods. But in our villages, everything is different; everything is authentic. Each object is made individually, the produce of human effort. For this reason, the things we make here are liked and admired more. What you see here, what you eat and drink here, represents the culture, craftsmanship and art of centuries. Outsiders, people from other countries, who know the importance of these things, have been visiting and exploring our mountains and villages and the products they buy here they take back to their own countries and produce them there.

"Today, many valuable products being sold in the world have been copied from the originals grown and produced here, in our country. For example, many remedies and medicines produced by the world's major pharmaceutical companies have taken advantage of the unique therapies once used here in

176

Anatolia. We've succeeded in destroying the most developed natural treatments methods, namely the *Lokman remedies*. We've stopped people from producing natural medicine but today we remain outside the world market."

Everyone was totally engrossed by what Güneş was saying: "This is something we can say absolutely clearly: Anatolian village culture is one of the world's greatest treasures. The reason for this is because this culture is an extraordinary accumulation of thousands of years of development. Thousands of villages in Anatolia have amassed this culture. It is impossible to come across a similar culture anywhere else in the world. It is due to this that we have devoted ourselves to protecting and developing village culture." These words had a huge impact on the audience; after all, Güneş was a well-educated and well qualified person!

Once again there was a vigorous round of applause. The young man's speech was deeply impressive. It was also thoughtful and well-considered. Regulations had been made that meant some villages had lost their identities, while others had disappeared altogether. A new place, called a neighbourhood in city-speak, had been created. Meanwhile, traditional Anatolian culture is at an increasing risk of destruction.

As the applause moderated, Ay approached the platform with Aygün, the village's most beautiful musician. Ay announced that Aygün was going to sing a türkü, a beautiful Turkish folk song. The time for entertainment had come! The words of Aygün's folk song echoed through the darkness and her sweet voice filled the night air, engulfing the audience in a wave of emotion.

Remember to fall in love...

You'll walk slowly down these ways,
As the sun sets blushingly,
Even if you're as blue as blue can be
You won't be feeling sad.
Don't forget you'll never be beaten,
You won't be bothered by the defeated ones
Remember that one day the sun will rise again,
Dimming egos, withered hopes
All will come into bloom again.
Don't be sad, cease your worrying
Stop your tears, scatter your sorrows.
Fear not! It's coming
To light our darkening world,
My sorrows, my fears disappear
And I'm loving again with excitement, with a thrill.

By the time Aygün left the stage, everyone was lost in their own private world. It was as if they were searching for something in the very depths of their souls...

At that very moment, a group of spirited folk dancers jumped onto the stage and just as quickly as it had come, the spell cast by Aygün's music was broken. The lively and irresistible, foot-tapping rhythm of the music made it impossible for the audience not to join in...

First the children and then the grownups jumped up to dance. The ground trembled and the mountains echoed with the music, dancing and singing that lasted long into the night.

It was as if the village was had been awoken by its own art, culture, excitement and love; quite literally, it had been born again.

The Autumn

Summer was well and truly over. When the first snows appeared on the mountains, there was another flurry of activity in the village. Due to the heavy snowfall in the region, roads could remain unpassable for long periods and some measures had to be taken to avoid food shortages. As a result, preparations for winter got underway at full speed.

The villagers would never forget this last summer. So many extraordinary innovations had happened in the village, from now on they would never be anxious about the winter months. The village was no longer as dead as a graveyard. It was as if everything had been reborn, even the animals looked bright-eyed and full of vitality.

Sis and his friends were still stitching away at the tailor's workshop they had established, working on the various commissions people had ordered. Another group were drying and packing fruit and vegetables in the Culture House. Preparations were underway for planting winter vegetables in the solar greenhouse. Due to increasing orders, the amount of homemade preserves and the production of cheese, butter and honey had increased. The villagers had begun to produce not only for their own needs; they were also marketing and selling their products.

The once sluggish and inactive life of the village was a thing of the past; there was now a new, lively and productive one instead. Some people who had left came back to the village and repaired their houses. However, the situation changed when a couple of people decided to demolish their old houses and replace them with reinforced concrete ones. When it became clear that persuasion wouldn't work, a meeting was hastily organised between the project committee and the village authorities during which two important decisions were made.

The first was to protect the village under the 'Village Protection and Improvement Plan', while the second was to declare the whole village an ecological zone. According to these decisions, all buildings must follow certain standards and designs and biodiversity would be protected in the region. No toxic or polluting chemicals could be used in agriculture. And all agricultural production would be natural. As a result, formal applications were made regarding these decisions and legal proceedings were begun.

With these decisions it was the first time in Turkey that a village had taking ownership of its own cultural values. The incident was leaked to the media and even reached the headlines. Several journalists interviewed professors who said they supported the project, while others filmed exchanges with Güneş, his friends, the Muhtar and the villagers.

In the national media, the most notable subject of debate was sun culture. People wanted to learn more about it and see it being used in the village. Therefore, the most visited places were the Culture Centre and the restored houses, both of which used solar architecture. Meanwhile, appropriate repairs, in line with solar architecture, were being carried out in some houses under the supervision of special teams.

Similarly, three master craftsmen established their own teams with five youngsters employed in each one. Furthermore, plans for repairs were being made by Güneş and his friends, who also watched over the process.

One notable success was that visitors were very keen to buy healthy sun-dried products. Most popular proved to be jars of sun-dried preserves, vegetables and the totally natural and exceptionally delicious *Tarhana soup*.

October was pretty busy. The winter products had already been prepared, the wood had been collected and the storage had been completed, but there were quite a few visitors, even a couple of foreigners. The village was now a popular and well-known curiosity, one that everyone wanted to see.

The Children of the Sun were so elated and so honoured. The had succeeded in a region, in an uncaring country, where rural life was neglected, forgotten and village culture was categorically on the way out.

The Interview

Yarkın Bey was one of the country's most famous journalists. He had come to the village to do some research and with the aim of interviewing the young friends and craftsmen who had put the solar project in an isolated village into practice. Tea and coffee were served in the Culture House, after which the interview began. The journalist asked his first question: "Why have you chosen a solar house and why in this village?"

Yarkın was pretty well informed about solar architecture and solar houses. There were already many examples of solar houses throughout the world, and they were becoming increasingly widespread. He'd seen and studied some experimental ones in Turkey: one designed by Professor Hakkı Ögelman and another built by METU were among the first. Later, more experimental houses were built and tested in Ankara, Izmir, Istanbul, as well as other places. However, the solar saving rates were not at the desired levels. But, why did the young friends want to make such a project in a village? It was beyond his comprehension.

Ay, who enjoyed acting, especially when she had an audience, replied to this question eloquently but also with a hint of sarcasm: "Because this is our village." Ay's answer surprised the journalist but she hadn't finished: "Yes, we had to think long and hard before we decided on our own village. It is quite normal, isn't it? It wouldn't have seemed right somehow to do a project in another village, while our village is still here." Gök spoke up: "Yes, that's right. We chose our village. As people who were born and grew up here, we know lots about these houses. You can only do a good job if you possess the right information. That's why we selected our familiar village.

Su began to speak; her voice clear, her speech fluent: "Like you, we researched various solar houses. Something attracted our attention. An issue discussed widely in books about solar town planning and solar architecture with which we totally agree, is that modern architecture is a style based on fossil fuels and one that has turned its back on the sun. In short, modern architectural models are not compatible with solar architecture styles. Whatever you do, you won't get a positive result." The journalist's astonishment was clear; he hadn't yet read the books she'd mentioned, but this interpretation was very interesting. "How's that?" he asked. "Are you saying these modern buildings are being constructed without taking the environment and climate conditions into account?"

"Unfortunately, that's exactly the case," said Su. "Are you able to show me one modern building design that takes climate into account, or takes the sun into consideration? Regardless of where houses are built – on mountains, in valleys, near the coast, inland, in hot areas or in cold, they're all exactly the same style, the same kind of building. For this reason alone, modern building designs shouldn't be acknowledged as an authentic architectural style. It seems to me that this type of architecture has been developed as a kind of lure, a devious way to increase consumption and expand the use of fossil fuels."

The journalist was thoroughly confused. What was it he'd heard about modern architecture in a forgotten mountain village thousands of metres high? It was as if Doğa guessed what the journalist was thinking: "OK, you heard right. It's true. Modern architecture has turned its back on the sun, so it requires masses of energy." By now the journalist was totally speechless, at a loss for words. Could this system, one used across the entire planet, be wrong and based on falsehoods?

183

Güneş offered a different perspective to support his friends. "Actually, it's not so surprising. In a society where everything's made for consumption, buildings must, by necessity, also be commodities where consumption takes place rather than merely for accommodation. Buildings by default, must use up large amounts of water, nature and energy." It was true. In fact, there had been much criticism along these lines for a long time. Finding his voice again, the journalist returned to the subject of the village. "But the solar house you've built here, is it in keeping with the village's architectural style?"

"Of course, it is, very much so," replied Güneş. "The village houses you see have been built using a very different approach from the modern buildings made for consuming energy. For thousands of years, villages had to create the conditions for survival, so they developed their own cultures. Because villages are productive, they developed productive systems.

"In the days before coal and oil, villagers had no option other than to heat their homes using solar energy or wood. As a result, they could evaluate the local energy potential of their village very well. To begin with, they developed the means of production and created suitable living spaces using the sun. They formed heating and cooling systems using the sun; so much so, that they managed to develop systems that heat during the winter and cool during the summer."

"My goodness," the journalist exclaimed. "You've really been inspired by this culture, haven't you?" Güneş responded to this immediately: "Absolutely we have! Village sun culture has inspired us, and it's shown us the way. We've benefited a great deal from all this accumulated knowledge; cultural accumulation, if you like. The villagers managed to do it in the past, so why can't we do it now?

184

"Incidentally, during our research, we also examined different solar cultures in Anatolia under different climate conditions. In each climatic zone we observed that the sun and climate characteristics were also different. So, production and architectural forms also differ. We've tried to benefit from all these practices and to give them a modern identity."

"So, what you're saying is that this solar house you've developed in this village has been achieved by applying these thousands of years of cultural accumulation?" "That's it, exactly. We've taken into consideration the solar properties of the houses, supported with new technology and increased the efficiency of the solar energy. In using this method, we thought that we could contribute to the culture of solar architecture."

"Well, if what you're saying is right, why don't other people use this culture or develop efficient solar systems?"

"These things take time. So far, Turkey hasn't developed a policy on solar architecture. The political powers need to look at the issues sympathetically, to make the legal framework and regulations and to create the necessary incentives. It looks as if it could all take quite a while."

Güneş sighed deeply before continuing: "But, some sympathetic architects have been studying solar cultures from the past and using it to develop contemporary models in their designs. It's just unfortunate that there are so few of them. All that usually happens is that mass produced solar panels and collectors are placed on the roofs. But this is just a small part of what's needed. Real solutions can only be possible if there's serious advances in solar cities and architecture."

"Do you think the examples you're making could galvanise politicians, administrators and the responsible organisations?"

"That we can't know. But we do believe that villagers will take possession of their own culture, revive their villages and produce natural products and that they'll benefit enormously from them." The journalist had come to his last question: "How will the villagers manage to do these things on their own? Do they have sufficient resources to do all this?"

It was Ay who answered: "Don't forget, we are also villagers and if we can, they can. They can ask us or the universities for help if they want. But they probably won't need to. Over the centuries, our rural folk, who have developed and practiced the most advanced, most diverse solar cultures in the world, have overcome every kind of difficulty and survived. They will be able to do the same this time too."

When the interview was over and it was time to leave, the journalist thanked Güneş and his companions. As he was leaving, he recalled Ay's encouraging and loyal words: "...we are also villagers and if we can, they can."

Eco-tourism

The increasing number of visitors coming to the village required new measures to be taken.

On arrival, visitors would first drop by the village house for refreshments – tea or coffee. Then they would chat with the locals. When asked where they would like to stay in the village and with whom, things could become rather confused and problems arose. As a result, the Children of the Sun set about organizing a meeting.

Gök spoke first: "People coming to the village don't know what they're supposed to be doing and have difficulties with accommodation. We need to find a solution." Su explained this problem in more detail: "Foreigners, in particular, who can't speak our language, are having even more trouble. They're at a complete loss to know what to do here in the village."

"I think the action that began in our village has been picked up by the foreign media," Doğa noted. "It seems likely that by next year the number of foreign tourists will have increased even further. But there are only a very few people in the village who can speak a foreign language. We need to find a solution for this as soon as we can."

Gök had an idea: "Everyone in our group speaks a foreign language. For the time being, maybe the foreign tourists could be directed to us, so we can deal with them." Everybody agreed. This sounded like a good idea, but Ay wasn't so sure: "You're right of course. This could certainly offer a short-term solution. But there are bound to be times in the future we're busy, so this requires some more permanent and comprehensive solutions. I think we need to build a much more serious tourism infrastructure for this."

"Yes," said Gök. "To me, there should be some kind of tourism organization. But what kind of organization, what kind of tourism? It wouldn't be a subject that our villagers could do much to sort out."

It was Doğa who offered a concrete proposal: "I don't think the foreigners that come to our village are typical tourists. I think the kind of people coming here are more likely to be nature lovers and people who are interested in different cultures, so the kind of tourism we should consider establishing here should be rural, or eco-tourism. It's the sort of tourism that's developing really rapidly at the moment and there's no reason why we shouldn't have it in this village, too."

This was absolutely true. Eco-tourism had spread so fast across the world in recent years, it had already become one of the main forms of tourism in many countries. And Turkey was a large country with a vast range of eco-tourism opportunities. If they could develop a suitable eco-tourism model for this village, it could be used for other villages as well.

Su, who had studied abroad and could speak several foreign languages, now shared her ideas: "I get many messages from abroad; from student groups, from universities. They're all saying that they would like to come here to learn about and study our village's culture and natural environment. I think we should give priority to those who would like to research the natural and cultural wealth of our village."

Güneş, who had maintained his silence from the outset, had heard enough. Now it was his turn to speak: "Yes, you are all right. But – and it's a big but – although we shouldn't forget that tourism can be thought of as an important source of income for the development of the village, we should also consider the possibility that it can also be dangerous. We should not ignore the fact that our village has its own unique values and while organizing this activity we must ensure these are protected. This has to be our fundamental principle."

This was the right approach. Mass tourism had spread to virtually every part of the country's coastline and the natural environment was being destroyed and plundered. Much of the coastline and seashores had been concreted, with the result that the wildlife and ecological balance was, to a large extent, destroyed. And this situation was not limited to the coasts: mountain and highland tourism had resulted in these places becoming swamped by massive amounts of concrete.

Everyone understood the problem. The Children of the Sun could start work on developing an eco-tourism model that was specific to the village, and that considered its unique characteristics.

To begin with the team decided to research and discuss the concept of sojourn culture in eco-tourism. This culture was a rich one that had been in existence for millennia. The origins of this culture are rooted in ancient humanistic thinking, and later in the *Masnavi* and *Bektashi* philosophies. Villagers would have been cast and developed in this cultural tradition. Each villager would have been proud to accommodate people they didn't know and share their last chunk of bread with them. This profound humanistic philosophy is a culture that must be kept alive.

Güneş and his friends would never give way to western style tourism, which is alien to Turkish culture and harms both it and nature equally. They would try to revive the ancient Anatolian *konukluk* philosophy and live and work with this instead.

There was another reason to make this decision. During the summer internships, students had stayed with families in the village and had developed genuine relationships with them. They'd done some household chores together; they'd learned to prepare dishes they'd never heard of; they'd prepared delicious pastes and purees using organic products; they'd worked in the vineyards, orchards and gardens.

They'd harvested fruit and vegetables and dried them in the sun. It was an extraordinary time for the students; one in which they gain practical experience of life, something that they'd never come across until then. The sad and emotional scenes on their departure were also indications of the strong ties that had been established between the villagers and the students. So, this tradition of hospitality – this sojourn culture – should be enriched and kept alive.

There was another interesting dimension: the villagers were also the hosts. They were the people who accommodated their guests and in doing so taught them about this culture. The guests were the ones who learned. It would be impossible to find this kind of relationship in western style tourism. Here in the village there was no concept of a guest-servant type relationship. This was a different type of tourism based on sharing and cooperation, one in which love, and respect was the result. [10]

They remembered the words of Atatürk to the British king: "I have taught my nation everything, but I could not teach them servitude!" According to Güneş and his friends, the villagers should not wait on those who were staying in their homes. Household chores must be shared or done together.

---

[10] *The project mentioned here has been tried and tested many times jointly by the Ürünlü Cultural Village Project and METU academics and positive results were obtained. It was recommended as an eco-tourism model by academics who implemented this research. (Internet search: Ürünlü village cultural project.)*

Of course, this form of accommodation – sojourn – would also provide an economic return.

After all, isn't this kind of eco-tourism an opportunity for people who are interested in village life and culture? Also, isn't the aim of such a project to support people who live in rural areas and provide them with employment? And finally, don't people who come for eco-tourism holidays already know that unlike mass tourism it's necessary to get on with their hosts and the other villagers and learn about the culture, biodiversity and everything necessary to survive in such a village?

For all these reasons, eco-tourism is ideally suited to the hospitality culture, which is one of the most important traditions of the village and it was something they could start immediately. Güneş and his friends met up with the people who would be opening their homes to guests and explained the system to them. "You will be hosting your guest, but you should never ask them for money. The money from this tourism will be transferred to the fund and, after calculating the expenses, you'll be given the rest."

Both the young friends and the villagers were overjoyed. They could easily open their rooms to guests. This eco-tourism was an important development. The villagers loved these young people and together they opened a new way of protecting their culture and employment. What more could they wish for?"

Now, all they had to do was launch this system. The young companions shared the tasks between them. They visited the houses one by one. They learned the names of those families who wanted to host the guests and the contracts were signed. The management of this job was distinct from the village house.

Meanwhile, the villagers created a website that covered village culture, nature, history and family life in the village. On these pages there was also specific information relating to solar culture and its activities.

Applications would be made using the internet and accommodation would be allocated from the cultural centre. The villagers themselves would not be dealing with financial matters directly with their guests. This would be under the authority of Güneş and the Children of the Sun. In short, the villagers would be making money but indirectly.

The whole village lived happily with the new project.

Chapter 8

A solar revolution in the village

A solar oven

Ay, Doğa and Su were walking along the road, chatting about events in the village. Pausing in front of the blacksmith's shop, which had only recently reopened, they spotted Güneş and the blacksmith, Yusuf Usta, sitting chatting. Yusuf Usta saw them. Beckoning them over, he said: "Hey girls. Why not join us for tea?"

The young women hastened into the shop, which was rather cramped. Yusuf Usta had reopened the old shop at the request of the Children of the Sun. He had inherited it from his father but didn't really know what to do with it. The knives and copper pots that had been produced there in the past should really be made again, but there weren't that many people who still wanted to buy such things. Güneş had been planning to discuss this issue with the blacksmith and now the girls had joined them in the shop, it seemed a good time to raise the subject.

"You're right... Traditional pots and pans aren't really being used any more but, as you know, we're trying to revive the old village culture. More often than not it's the tourists who ask for these kinds of things, especially the handmade copper products. There's no reason why you couldn't produce similar ones here. Yusuf Usta smiled warmly and thanked him. "But" said Güneş, "There's something else we'd like you to do." "Certainly, Mr Güneş... Of course, it would be my pleasure," the craftsman said, not without a little curiosity. Yusuf Usta's sincere words rather impressed the young women.

Ay asked him: "As far as I'm concerned, you should start making solar equipment." The craftsman was rather surprised by her remark: "What do you mean? I don't know how to make solar equipment!" "I'm sure you do! You're the finest craftsman in this neighbourhood, you can do anything!" Doğa reassured him. "I think, you should make a solar oven and a solar stove. We need these in the village." Ay agreed: "Yes, yes, absolutely! A solar shower system could be interesting, too.

Ay's words caught everyone's imagination. A solar oven certainly, possibly a solar stove, but it was the first time they'd heard of a *solar shower system*. She explained what she meant and concluded by saying: "I think a solar shower system should be developed as this is something the village really needs." In the shop there was a blacksmith's forge and bellows. Next to this there was a small table. They were now all sitting around this table. This was an issue they would have to discuss in detail.

Water pipe systems were installed in the houses; however, water used in the home couldn't be used for watering the garden, if it was dirty. Güneş explained that to begin with a solar shower system would be installed in the garden of the village house and explained how it would be done. They would build a wooden hut; black pipes would be put on the roof and these would be covered with glass. One end of the pipe would be connected to a water tank the other one would be connected to the shower.

It took a while for Yusuf Usta to get his head around the idea but eventually he succeeded. Soon, he'd managed to install a solar shower system. Ay was the first to try it out, and as she stepped from the shower cabin, she was smiling: "Yeeees!" she squealed with excitement. "It's a wonderful feeling and

194

one I thoroughly recommend to everyone!" This was a simple but important task – and they'd done it. What's more, the shower water didn't go to waste. It was used to water the plants and trees in the garden.

It was almost evening. The villagers were chatting in the square. The main topic was the solar shower system. They were all wondering if they could manage to install one too, in their own gardens. Of course, everybody who wanted one could build one, so the blacksmith Yusuf Usta did not remain unemployed for long.

"Are there no resources for us women?" They heard a voice and looked in the direction of where it was coming from. The voice belonged to Hatice Teyze. She continued: "Even during the summer, we have to burn wood to do the cooking. Apart from the smoke, we're overwhelmed by the heat... Aren't there any remedies for us women?" As one, the villagers' gaze turned towards Güneş and his friends. "Sure, there are!" said Doğa, "The remedy you're looking for is called a solar oven, or a solar stove."

Güneş explained in more detail: "There are lots of solar ovens and stoves in the world. But none of them run efficiently. We're currently working on a suitable model and after we've finished, we'll share our project with you." Although the Children of the Sun had been working on the same project for a long time, they weren't yet sure how to explain it. They would have to speed up their work.

They worked on the project for a while longer but still hadn't found one that was suitable. Ay, who was a good designer, asked her friends for some extra time to carry out intensive research of her own. They agreed to her request. Following this, Ay locked herself away in the house and was not seen for quite a while.

195

One day she suddenly appeared holding a bunch of papers and what looked like a parcel in her hands. "All right everyone, the jobs done!" she announced. Her friends assumed that they would be going to see Yusuf Usta. "No," she said." We have to see the carpenter, İbrahim Usta, first. Right now, in fact." And that's where they went. As soon as Ay had shown him the parcel in her hands she announced: "Now our solar oven is ready."

When they'd opened it, they saw a wooden box and on opening that they saw another, on top of which was a glass cover. The inside of the box was covered in black metal. This was a miniature version of what would eventually be the real thing. Everybody wondered how and if it was going to work. They would only see the result after it had been tested.

They put a small container in the black box that they'd filled with water. They then placed the box in direct sunlight. As the sun rose higher in the sky, the temperature would increase. They closed the glass cover and began to wait. About 12 minutes later the water had reached boiling point. Everyone jumped for joy, thrilled that the test had been successful. They had launched a new cooking method, simply by using the sun's energy.

They tested the solar oven in different ways. They cooked rice, soup and pasta. The cooking time was as much as double or triple that of a gas oven, but what more could they ask for?

On hearing this news, people came to the village house. There, they were able to see the system up close and congratulate the youngsters on their success. The number of people who wanted a similar stove increased, so now İbrahim Usta the carpenter would have lots of work.

Meanwhile, the days were passing rapidly, and a fierce, chill wind had begun to blow through the village. It was almost winter. The hardest days of the year were approaching both for the villagers and the Children of the Sun. Now they would learn whether their projects were a success or a disappointing failure.

Midwinter

The winters were always hard in this village. By October the first snows had fallen on the mountains and by November the village was covered too. Everywhere was snowy.

Güneş and his companions had been looking forward to the winter rather impatiently. They were curious to learn whether their projects would work. For this reason, they installed sensors in the traditional village houses. They were going to measure the temperatures and record them. These reports would enable them to look at the contrasting levels of heat and humidity in the summer and the winter months. They could then compare these with those of the other modern houses and determine the efficiency of the solar system.

Once they began to get the details they met once a week to discuss them. They assessed the first readings in December and were pleased with them. Everything was going well. The seedlings started to sprout in the greenhouses and the manufacturing in the workshops were continuing pretty well too. They visited some of the houses that had been built to take advantage of the sun. They spoke with people who were living in those houses. Everyone was happy. They also visited Orhon Usta and Emine Teyze.

Emine Teyze brought up the subject at once: "We're really pleased. We used to have to light such a lot of wood to get warm but now we don't. Since it started to snow, we've also begun to use the stove from time to time. Before, we only used to heat one room and we had to stay in it all winter. We don't know what you've done but this fire becomes warm with only a small amount of wood and it heats the whole building. Thank you so much for everything you've done."

They studied all the measurements carefully and looked at the amount of wood being used. They could see that energy consumption had decreased by about 80%.

Daily life in winter was the typical routine. But one day everything changed with a very unexpected event. There had been an avalanche over in the neighbouring village and some youngsters who had been visiting were buried underneath it. This potential tragedy was very alarming for everyone. A rescue team was organized, and they headed off to the village to see what could be done.

The youngsters who had been staying in a mountain house were trapped under the fallen snow. The rescue team started to dig tunnels, one from each side. After tunnelling for what seemed like ages, they finally managed to reach the chimney of the house. They carefully cleared the snow covering the chimney and finally, the rescue team managed to reach the place where they assumed the young people would be. But it was only when they heard their cries that they finally understood for certain that the youngsters were alive.

Even so, their survival had not been without a struggle. Fortunately, they had not frozen, thanks to the blankets and quilts in the house; however, they had used up all the food and they'd begun to run short of oxygenated air. Trapped in this way they were expecting the inevitable, tragic ending. As a result, hearing the words, "Hello friends!" echo down the chimney from Güneş and the other rescuers, made them feel as if they had been born again. What unbelievable joy they felt! The opened chimney allowed them to breathe in the fresh, cold air. They felt even better when food and drink was lowered down to them via the chimney stack.

Their parents had already arrived at the scene of the avalanche and were obviously anxious. But their happiness on learning that their children were safe was definitely a sight worth seeing. They were beyond delighted! There was also a TV crew broadcasting live news of the rescue. They were making interviews with people involved from time to time. Meanwhile, the good news was conveyed to the governor and a search and rescue helicopter he'd arranged to be sent arrived at the scene.

The casualties, two boys and a girl, were university students. They're plan had been to climb to the "the peak of the gods" but they had begun their hike without informing the villagers. Walking in the snow had exhausted them, so before climbing the mountain, they had decided to spend the night in the mountain house. "What were your feelings when you first became aware that you'd been trapped under the avalanche?" asked the TV reporter. "Well, of course, we were really scared. We didn't know what to do. We tried to find a solution, but we couldn't. There was nothing we could do except wait."

"So, how did you spend your days under the snow?" continued the reporter. "well, at first, it wasn't a problem; we were all healthy. We sometimes opened the window to get snow to melt and drink. But when our supplies had finished, the situation changed completely. In the end, our main problem was the lack of oxygen. Breathing became really difficult. If the rescue team hadn't arrived when they did, we could well have died."

Together with the villagers, Güneş and his friends had successfully taken part in the rescue. They were treated almost like national heroes and not only were they being asked about the rescue but also about the projects they'd made in the village. They patiently answered all of them; after all, this was an opportunity to spread news of solar culture all over the country.

The villagers looked after the rescued students in their houses. After they'd rested, they took buses back to their hometowns. But before leaving the village they thanked the villagers and the team who'd rescued them. They said that they'd never forget this village, nor the villagers, especially Güneş and his friends. The sincerity of their heartfelt thanks was unmistakeable. Of course, being trapped under metres of snow like that had been a terrible experience for the youngsters but even so it had resulted in some good outcomes for the village.

Thanks to this news, the villagers had been given a chance to be heard and become even more well-known. The number of tourists visiting the village increased even further and it helped eco-tourism become even more popular.

One day, while the villagers were chatting in the village house, Su entered: "There's loads of interest for next season, so much I think it'll be impossible for everyone to come here." Su was aware of the situation and the limited resources and knew this interest could actually result in problems. She explained that there could well be environmental and cultural problems. Perhaps it would be possible to host some of the visitors at other nearby villages. As a result, the neighbouring villages also began to benefit from solar culture and its influences, too.

In the meantime, two new groups had arrived, and these attracted the villagers' attention. One group was from Japan and the other was from Germany. The Japanese government wanted to send a group of scientists to study Anatolian culture. The German students wanted to come and stay in the village under the leadership of a German expert, to study the highland culture. This group also wanted to renovate the yayla huts.

201

Their requests were welcomed with great interest. After all, for a long time, these kinds of things had been among their objectives. Now, these brilliant opportunities had landed at their feet and they were ones that should definitely not be missed.

Their job was done: this amazingly rich culture that had come from the depth of Anatolian history would be investigated and with its reintroduction it could, in the future, shed light on a civilization that was at one with both nature and the environment.

The Sun Revolution

One snowy day the Children of the Sun gathered together for a chat. Their earlier anxieties had gone, to be replaced by levels of happiness that made their faces glow. Outside the sun was shining; its light poured in through the windows. As a result, not only were their hearts warm, their bodies were too!

Güneş looked at his friends. Everybody looked happy. "You do know, don't you," he asked them, "how much remains to be done. For instance, there a loads of village houses waiting to be renovated." "You're right" said Gök. "I think we'll be able to start the house repairs in the spring." Ay remarked: "I think the construction companies we've spoken with will be able to manage the repairs of the old houses."

The repair of five buildings, including the village house, was now complete. The families who lived in these houses would be able to spend the winter in them without any problem. But the rest of the houses should also be ready for the following winter.

Su voiced a problem that had been concerning her: "The thing I've been most worried about is the village's electricity problems. Our winters are really hard, and you all know how many power cuts we get here. Most homes don't get electricity during the winter. Yes, we've solved the problem with the streetlights, but we've not found a solution for electricity in people's homes."

"I agree with Su," said Doğa. "Most families have problems because of these power cuts, and we need to find a way to solve this. And I have a suggestion!" A chorus of "Tell us, tell us," rang from the others. Doğa continued: "I think it is time to establish a power plant in the village."

She was right. Building a power plant in the village was really crucial. But how? It would be incredibly difficult to build one with only the village's resources and they had no idea how to find the kind of money they'd need for such a project. Even the government bought oil from abroad. Although there were rich resources, Turkey had long been dependent on other countries.

In the 1970s, the United States had imposed a fuel embargo on Turkey. There had been serious problems in the country, but it was a situation that had mostly impacted on the villages. It was clear that the time had come to find some substantial and serious solutions.

"I've got it…Listen to this!" said Gök. "There are many resources we can use here – this is a fact. After all, we have the mountains, the rivers, the wind. What's more, we've got masses of solar energy too. Why don't we use it?"

Meanwhile, Güneş was thinking about all this too. Gök was right. It was simply absurd not to use all these renewables. These resources were not only in his country but many others too. If the government chose, it could start energy production and the importing of energy could finally stop. He began to voice his ideas: "Let's try some alternative ideas. We could try to create a project that helps local people produce their own energy. Then, we could put it into practice."

Suddenly, a light began to shine in their eyes. Hadn't Güneş just mentioned a new model for producing energy? Güneş often made this sort of surprising speech. They looked at him with fascination, as he continued: "If you think about it, the energy models we speak about here in Turkey are ones that require huge investment, like nuclear power stations, coal-fired power plants, or ones that use natural gas. It means, the largest foreign corporations are going to be the organisations

204

that take on these projects, making heaps of money in the process – and of course, it's us who have to pay. Corporations like this have control over the entire world and there's only one way to get rid of this problem. And that is to find a way of producing our own energy." Güneş had certainly hit on a major problem. But changing the world order in such a short time would never happen.

Gök looked at his friend. Ordinary people, producing their own energy? Really? Such a thing seemed to be nothing more than an impossible dream. "I think perhaps we should find more realistic projects," he confessed. "For example, if we could get support from the government, we could establish a power plant using wind or water. Equally, these projects would also be possible if we were able to establish a solar power plant."

Güneş looked at his friend: "It's certainly possible," he acknowledged. "But although it may seem simple enough at first to establish such a power plant, when we think about it in detail, it would be really hard to carry the energy through-out the entire village. Each one of them would require a really massive undertaking and huge investments. And, as if this weren't enough, villagers would end up paying for it for their entire lifetimes… Personally, I think we should find simpler and more straightforward projects. It'd be better to find solu-tions that everybody can understand and do themselves."

Ay, who was sitting in a corner and watching them wisely but without saying a word, started to laugh: "You still don't understand, do you?" She was animated and her eyes were bright. "Güneş is talking about houses *that can produce their own energy*." "Ay's absolutely right!" exclaimed Güneş. "She's hit the nail on the head… We make buildings that can produce their own energy, like the cultural centre, the village house and the five other houses we've already done. If we

205

build all the houses in the same way, they can have their own independent energy. In other words, we won't need any power plants at all."

Ay continued from where she'd left off: "So, our village could be independent in terms of energy. We won't be reliant on either nuclear energy or oil anymore." It was Güneş' words that really caught his friends' imagination: "If we manage to pull off this project successfully, the Solar Revolution can begin in our village!"

The Children of the Sun all looked at each other. These words had really got them thinking. All of them were thrilled that they would be launching a new revolution, an energy revolution.

Thanks to the panels they had put on each house, they could produce electricity. Actually, the village would be a collection of small independent energy producing units. This was a totally different concept from other solar energy plants.

"Do you really think that every villager could produce their own energy and not fall into the trap of international monopolies and local collaborators. What is this if not revolutionary? The energy we'll be producing is cheap, local and easy to use. Our villagers can set up this system. It's straightforward and can be installed everywhere, gradually becoming widespread." "But..." said Su, "if it was so easy, why hasn't it been done already?"

Güneş continued, his voice increasingly passionate: "There are so many reasons why, Su. First and foremost, there's the collaboration between the nuclear and oil industries. They put a country's authorities under pressure. The second reason is the inadequacies in technological development. Then, the third reason is the emphasis given to planning and design that excludes the sun on architecture and city planning. And the fourth is having signed up to international dependency in the long term. The last reason is that there are still no legal regulations about it."

Almost shouting, Güneş said, "Just think everyone, nobody in our country's aware of its most important riches; especially, the government and the authorities." Su burst out: "Do you know, I'm having real difficulty in understanding the universities and researchers. Although our country has the richest solar culture in the world, our universities aren't doing enough research on it and never include it in their education and training programmes."

Doğa commiserated with her. "Yes... I am really ashamed of our politicians' short sightedness and lack of vision. They never think about anything apart from their own interests. In our country, which we all know is a country of the sun, not one political party has considered instigating solar legislation."

Despite all these negative issues, the Children of the Sun and the villagers were happy. They had managed to achieve many wonderful things; they had carried out successful solar projects and put them into practice. They truly believed that they had started a solar revolution. Now they were experiencing the joy, the happiness, of having done their job to the best of their ability and in the best way possible...

The Song of Rebirth

Ay finally remembered that famous poem she'd been thinking about. It begins with the lines:

There is a village far away
And that village is ours

This poem had been written a long time ago. Anatolian villages had already changed significantly. Now it was time to write a new version of the same poem. It was Ay who first recited these words. They eventually became the words of a beautiful song.

There is a village in Anatolia
That village is ours
But quietly, slowly, it began to disappear

Our hearts were weeping
It was not the skies above our village that became dark
It was our culture, our individuality
They were forsaking us, one by one

Heading into the darkness of Anatolia
The Sun entered our souls
Opening new ways, new hopes
Blind eyes started to see

Minds became enlightened
The Sun is all around us
Rising in all its glory
Bringing communities back to life
Filling hearts with hope and souls with love

Hand in hand the Sun and the Moon are in the heavens
All hail to them from Mother Earth
And from her people united in their strength

SON - THE END

Contact: cetingok@gmail.com

WhatsApp: +90 505 4066992

OTHER PUBLICATIONS BY THE AUTHOR

1: THE SUN RISES AGAIN

This book of 12 essays describes the relationship between the sun and life, humanity's interest in the sun and previously undocumented insights into this relationship. It also describes how people search for their inner selves and values. It conveys, in a straightforward way, the concept of "me" by changing it to "we" and helps us to discover other worlds within ourselves.

2: THE SUN CONSCIOUSNESS

A New Philosophy of Life

An original concept in every way, this book offers a whole new worldview and philosophy of life. Despite the artificial consciousness that contemporary philosophers have formed in terms of human awareness, this work shows the accurate and realistic core values of life. It explains the new philosophical principles of a new worldview, as real as it is natural. (204 pages)

3. SOLAR CITY

City Planning Based on Solar Energy

Together with technical information and examples, this book describes how people can use solar energy in the most effective way in living environments such as cities, mass housing and buildings. It explains the keyways to do away with environmental pollution. It is a reference book showing how solar cities can be planned and implemented.

4. ANATOLIAN SUN CIVILIZATION

A New Civilisation Project for Anatolia

Focusing on the Turkish Republic, the subject of discussion in this book is to establish a civilization beyond the west. Unfavourable developments in the world have provided a suitable environment for establishing a new civilization. These negative developments make it necessary for humanity to develop and apply a new system of values, new ideas, new technologies, new lifestyles and environments, and therefore a new civilization. Turkey is a country that has the skills and capabilities to enhance the new civilization the world needs and the country should urgently evaluate this opportunity.

5: GLOBAL WARMING AND SOLAR PROJECTS IN TURKEY

This book includes details of the studies, approaches and possible solutions with regard to environmental issues that we have been carrying out over the years in the planning department of the METU Faculty of Architecture. As well as being original, the projects discussed in the book include some distinctive features that pave the way for Turkey's advance towards new horizons. (192 pages)

6. SOLAR GREENHOUSES

Solar Energy Greenhouse Manual

This book describes the new greenhouse model that has been designed for the cold climate of central Anatolia, using solar energy. It explains about agricultural output, solar systems used in agriculture and greenhouse architecture. It also provides details about the collaborative work done by METU and Ankara University to solve problems. This model was

211

put into practice in Güneşköy near Ankara. The plants and solar systems located inside were tested. Production and applications are ongoing and the project in Güneşköy is open for visits. (173 colour pages)

7. SOLAR TOWNS AND THE SOLAR ARCHITECTURE

Planning Design Application

This is a reference book for people who would like to benefit from the sun. The book describes the core life values of the sun and its features, together with an introduction to the extraordinary features of solar energy. The most important feature of the book is that the future of the Sun civilization is on the way. It also helps to answer some questions, such as how are sun cities built? How is sun architecture put into practice?

With 200 colour pages and supported by numerous examples from around the world, this book provides examples of solar cities and solar architecture and offers a comprehensive evaluation of every aspect, from Sun philosophy to Sun culture.

NB: This is a reference book on solar-cities and solar campuses.

8. THE MYSTERIES OF THE SUN (A NOVELLA)

Where is the Mysterious Garden of the Sun? What secrets does it hide about nature and life? What do the young people see and discover in this *mysterious garden*? How do they access the information that sheds light on this age? How and why do they decide to build a solar civilization and bring the solar project to life? Through this book, the first to be written about solar culture, you will travel with the young people into a completely different world, discover the mysteries of the sun that are still unknown to this day, and begin to think about how you can contribute to this culture.

9. CULTURAL CITY OF ARINNA

A cultural project about the city of the ANATOLIAN SUN GODDESS.

Including information, analyses and discussions about the Cult of Arinna and the Hittite civilization, in Alacahöyük, Turkey

A workshop organized by Göksu and published by DSP

Publications:

I. Güneş ve Kent, (Sun & City) 1992, 2002,
II. Güneş Yeniden Doğuyor (The Sun is Reborn) (denemeler) 1998
III. Güneş Bilinci (Sun Consciousness) Yeni bir yaşam felsefesi (deneme) 2000
IV. Anadolu Güneş Uygarlığı (Anatolian Sun Civilisation) (Güneşe dayalı uygarlık (deneme).
V. Küresel Isınma Türkiye'nin Güneş Projeleri 2002 (Turkey's Global Warming Solar Project 2002) (araştırma)
VI. Güneş Kentler ve Güneş Mimarisi (Sun Cities & Solar Architecture) (referans kitabı) 2015
VII. Günsera: güneş enerjili sera (Günsera: solar energy greenhouses) Modeli, 2015
VIII. Güneşin Gizemli Bahçesi, Güneş Hikayesi (The Mysterious Garden of the Sun/A Story of the Sun) (Deneme) 2016
IX. Arinna Kültür Kenti Projesi, Cultural City of Arinna Project (Hatti Hitit Uygarlığı canlandırma Projesi). (Çalıştay org, kitap), (Hatti Hittite Civilization Renaissance Project). (Workshop, book)
X. Köroğlu Kültürünü Canlandırma Projesi çalıştay org (Anadolu Efsanelerini canlandırma Projesi) Çalıştay, kitap org)/ Cultural Regeneration Project, workshop (Project for revitalizing Anatolian Legends) Workshop, book)
XI. Antalya – Ürünlü Kültür Köyü Projesi, Antalya – Ürünlü Village Cultural Project (Araştırma/research, kitabı/book)
XII. Bolu-Mudurnu Köyleri, ekoturizm projesi Çalıştay - Bolu/Mudurnu Villages – Ecotourism Project workshop
XIII. Kümelenmiş Kentsel Sistemler, Urban Cluster Systems (Ar-Ge/R&D, Planlama Modeli/Planning model)
XIV. Türkiye'de Kentsel Standartlar, Urban Standards in Turkey (ortak ar-ge/joint R&D, 3 cilt/3 volumes)